Scarlet Assassin

Scarlet Assassin

ISABELLA

WRITING AS
JETT ABBOTT

SAPPHIRE BOOKS

SALINAS, CALIFORNIA

Cover Design by Christine Svendsen
Editor - Lisa Boeving
Interior Designer - LJ Reynolds

Sapphire Books
Salinas, CA 93912
www.sapphirebooks.com

Printed in the United States of America
First edition – February 2014

Dedication

To the woman who never questions, why.
My love, Schileen.

Thomas, Eric and Alex, my heart!

Acknowldegements

Sometimes, no, isn't the end of journey, but the beginning of one. At least it was for me and I have the readers to thank for accompaning me on my travels.

To the readers who kept asking for another Jett Abbott book, thank you! Now you know my secret!

To my beta reader, Erin Saluta - your insight into the story was thought provoking and right on target. Thank you.

To my editor, Lisa Boeving - you keep me honest when I want to be lazy. Many thanks.

To Peggy Adams for finding all my flaws, a huge thanks for joining us at Sapphire Books.

To the wonderful women at Sapphire Books - you are amazing storytellers. When I grow-up I want to be just like you!

Chapter One

Selene sat entranced as the scratched and grainy images popped on the old, by-gone era theater. Built in the early 1900's, it still had all the smells of stale food, mold, and body odor that assaulted her senses as she kept her eyes glued to the images playing out before her. Her phone vibrated in her pocket as the scene continued to unfold, glowing in the darkness of the theater. She was tempted to ignore it. Whoever it was had intruded on her time and she had so little to herself lately.

Her jaw clenched. The longer the phone vibrated the angrier she got. Clearly, the caller wasn't getting the message. Her phone settings would prevent the caller from leaving a message for a reason. She didn't like talking to people. The phone was a necessary evil she had accepted on her terms. Finally, the vibration stopped and she lost herself once again in the silent film she had seen at least a hundred times. "Gish the dish" as she liked to refer to the silent film star, had enthralled her from an early age.

"One piece of that candy and you had to go back to the dish for more." A gentleman sitting next to her had said when the film premiered.

He was right. Selene had returned to see the film many times and would continue to do so for the length of her life, she was sure. Watching the DVD couldn't compare to the big screen setting. The larger than life images reminded her of a different time in her life and she could almost smell the hot popcorn, the heady rush of perfume, and the warmth of the woman she first saw the film with. She closed her eyes and laid her head back on the seat, memories flooding her mind.

It was her first time seeing a "moving picture" as they called it back then. World War I raged on another continent, rationing was common, work was hard, the hours long and days off were few and far between.

"Oh, I can't wait to see this. I heard the girls talking about it at work," her date said, pulling on her elbow, stopping her progress down the dirty, dark street. "I'm so glad you finally decided to take a night off, Selene. This should be fun."

The giddiness from Mavis was contagious. Selene rarely got excited, but it was hard not to as she watched her date. Smiling at the sheer joy on her companion's face, she grabbed her by the hand and started towards the theater. The smell of popcorn from the vendor sitting in front of the theater wafted through the air, greeting the movie patrons the closer they got.

"It's all the rage in New York. I hear the Ziegfeld Follies might have to shut down. No one's going to the shows now that moving pictures are here," Selene said, gettting caught up in the moment.

"Oh what a shame that would be. Don't you think?"

"Well, nothing lasts forever. Eventually things change."

"I suppose you're right." Mavis pulled Selene's arm. "Come on let's get a good seat. I don't want to miss one minute,"

One more turn and they would be on the lit street

of the movie theater, but something, someone, moved in the darkness next to Selene. Instinctively Selene leaned close to Mavis's ear.

"Don't turn around. Go straight to the movie theater and wait for me."

"What?" Mavis whispered.

"Don't turn around, we're being followed. Run to the theater and don't look back."

"But—"

"Save me some cracker jacks, now RUN!"

Selene was grabbed from behind and spun around. A slap across her face momentarily stunned her.

"You shouldna done that, now I gotta chase her down," a low voice husked out.

The rank smell of tobacco almost made Selene puke as she was struck again, this time with a closed fist. The tinny taste of blood filled her mouth while her body tensed with rage.

"You're gonna be so sorry you did that, asshole." Selene grabbed her attacker's hand. The bones of his knuckles ground together as she squeezed tighter. With a twist, she wrenched his hand over until his wrist snapped. He fell to his knees cursing.

"You bitch! Ya broke ma hand. I'm gonna kill ya."

"I don't think you're in a good position here, buddy," Selene snarled. Her fangs popped.

"What the fuck?"

"You should've really decided to do something more productive than molest two women going to the movies."

"Let me go and I'll leave you and the lovely lady alone. Look, I got a family to feed...kids." He pleaded his case.

"You should have thought about that before. I can't let you live now." Selene's nails lengthened and bit into his hand, anchoring him to her.

"Argghh." He screamed loud enough that she was sure someone would come to investigate. Pulling him behind some discarded wooden boxes, she cupped her hand over his mouth, muffling his scream. One swift lunge and she was on his neck, draining the life out of him. Finished, she dropped to her knees and suddenly felt nauseous. Gagging, she tried to stop herself from throwing up but her stomach revolted at the sour taste of his blood.

"Christ, he's a fucking drunk and a doper." Selene turned his arm over, looking for the telltale signs of drug use. He probably drank it with his alcohol. Medicinal of course. Waiting for the queasiness to stop, she stood and looked around, making sure no one had seen them slip behind the boxes. Throwing a few on top of him to cover his body, she tucked her shirt back into her trousers, pulled the cuffs of her sleeves down and straightened her jacket before returning to her date waiting for her at the ticket office.

Selene's vibrating cell phone yanked her from her memory. Pissed, she pulled it from her pocket so hard she almost ripped her pants. Her eyes narrowed when she recognized the caller ID. She jabbed at the screen.

"This better be important," she hissed.

An old man in front of her turned around, but before he could say anything Selene let out a low ominous growl.

"Don't growl at the nice humans, Selene."

"How do you know I'm not growling at you, AJ?"

AJ chuckled and continued, "Are you busy?"

"What the fuck do you want?"

"Are you busy?"

"Yes."

"Clarissa wants you to come over for dinner."

"Again?" Selene grabbed her grumbling stomach. Clarissa's last gastric creations weren't bad, Selene just wasn't sure she was ready to go all-carnivorous quite yet.

"Yep and she specifically asked me to invite you. So, Thursday at six p.m."

"I'm busy."

"Okay, Wednesday same time."

Selene could tell by the tone in AJ's voice that the kidding was over and it was no longer a request.

"Look, I might work for you but you don't own me. Is that clear?"

The man in front of Selene turned as her voice grew louder. This time she flashed a set of fangs and let out a low rumble. Selene smelled urine and felt a tad sorry for the old guy.

"You're not my master, AJ."

"I'm not asking for me, I'm asking for Clarissa."

"Fine, tell Clare I'll be there on Wednesday." *Might was well get it over with.*

"Clare?"

"Yeah?"

"Since when do you call my wife, Clare?"

"Since she told me to, why? I'm sure you have lots of other things you call her that she likes better. Like, Sweetheart, Honey, Sweetie Pie, Sugar Lips, shit like that."

"Well yeah, but she's never told me to call her Clare."

Selene could feel the fingers of jealousy reaching

through the phone and thread around her neck. *Calm down AJ Shit, she's your wife for Christ's sake.*

"Don't tell me to calm down."

Selene shook her head, she forgot AJ's telepathic abilities were greater than hers and she would have to sensor her thoughts around AJ.

"If you're jealous of Clarissa and my history, I guess I won't come over. Either that, or you'll have to deal with it. Besides, I have plenty to keep me busy at the club and hunting down leads on De Marcus."

"No, no it's fine."

Selene heard AJ strumming her fingers, a sign she was frustrated.

"I'm just…I'm just worried about Clarissa, that's all. Until we get De Marcus, I'll always be worried."

"We can talk about this tomorrow. Like I said, I'm right in the middle of something." Selene slammed the phone shut.

The lights and darks of the black and white film flicked across Selene's pale complexion as she immersed herself back into the movie

"Fine, tomorrow then."

Her target sat two rows in front of her. He'd been giving the wrong someone trouble and Selene was the solution to the problem. She could smell his fancy perfume, the gel he wore in his hair and the B negative coursing through his veins. Selene noticed the old man in front of her had decided to leave. Lucky for him, otherwise she would have had to shorten his time on this earth, too. Slipping up one row, she settled herself and watched the movie again. Things had picked up for her recently and she wasn't quite sure why, but she never passed up a job. More money got her closer to her goal of chucking it all and finishing her mountain retreat. It was so far off the beaten path, she relished her time alone there. The solitude, the clean air, the quiet made her nostalgic for another time, another place. Letting the memories slip away was probably best. She didn't need another walk down memory lane during a job. She needed her wits and speed, both of which were affected when she let the melancholy creep in.

Sliding over the seat directly behind the man, she caught a full whiff of him. Vampire! That's why she'd been called. The bastard wasn't just anyone; he also wasn't someone to be taken lightly. *Great! Why do these clients lie?* He'd probably heard her twenty minutes ago when she growled at the man, who wet himself. *Beautiful.*

Pulling her garrote, she unwound the thin piano wire, grabbed the handles, and sat quietly for a moment. She studied the size of his neck, his position in the seat and noticed his ears perk, just a bit. She'd have to be quick. Without a second of hesitation, she wrapped the long wire around his neck and pulled. He'd managed to get a couple of fingers between his neck and the wire, but it wouldn't matter. Putting her knee against the seat, Selene leaned back and yanked. She felt the digits stop her progress for a moment and then the resistance was gone. She'd cut right through them. Now she needed to be quick to finish the job. Pulling harder, she leaned back more and pushed both knees against the seat. A growl escaped the man's lips and she knew he was trying to shift into his vampire form.

"No doing, big guy," she said, switching handles from hand-to-hand and scissoring the garrote. So focused, a snap, a squish and the ping of the garrote as the wire straightened were the only sounds. She took a deep breath, taking in the aroma of fresh blood sprayed on her starched white shirt. Selene groaned as the heady smell engulfed and enflamed her. With a quick flick of her tongue, she wiped the garrote clean and wound it up, slipping the deadly instrument back into her pocket. She settled back and focused on the movie, her job done.

Chapter Two

S he's coming."
"Oh good. I've missed her. We haven't seen much of Selene since she left with De Marcus. Do you think she's avoiding us?" Clarissa stirred a pot, the steaming aroma filling the room.

AJ walked up to her wife, grabbing her hips and rubbing herself against Clarissa's tight ass. She would never miss an opportunity to touch Clarissa now that they were finally together. Clarissa stiffened and leaned against her chest.

"Is that all you think about?" Clarissa laid her head back on AJ's shoulder, giving her just enough room to snip at Clarissa's neck.

"Not all the time."

"Hmm?"

"Okay, most of the time. But can you blame me? I have a lot of catching up to do."

"How lucky for you the semester is almost over and you can have me all to yourself."

"Yes." AJ licked the throbbing vein, ready to burst. The pulse pulled AJ's incisors, an audible pop as they dropped ready for action. "I am lucky. I can't wait to keep you in bed all night and day. I think about making wild passionate love to you, feeding your heart and your soul." Pulling Clarissa closer, she grazed her points down Clarissa's neck, barely pricking the skin. Flicking her tongue across the slight bead of blood, her heart thumped so hard in her chest she knew Clarissa could hear it.

Hungry, my love?

Starving. AJ's thoughts were overpowering. She closed her eyes and concentrated on controlling her appetite.

What am I going to do with you?

Make love to me.

AJ's empathic abilities intensified as her connection to Clarissa got stronger. They felt each other, even when great distances apart. AJ knew Clarissa was working to bring them closer. She'd had a lot to overcome, thinking at first that AJ had been the one to kill her family, only to discover that De Marcus had in fact done it to keep Clarissa closer to him. De Marcus was evil personified even a hundred years ago. He'd taken advantage of his relationship with Clarissa's father and wormed his way into the family. Finally, he turned Clarissa when she was at her sickest, and AJ wondered how harsh her life with De Marcus had been. She'd gotten bits and pieces when they were quiet after their love making, but she'd had to be strategic with the questions. Clarissa had withdrawn when AJ inquired the first time, a sign she wasn't ready to talk about the past. While they had an eternity to explore the world and their pasts, AJ wanted De Marcus dead now so Clarissa could live.

"What are you thinking about?" Clarissa turned in AJ's arms and cradled her face.

AJ's eyes softened. Looking down at Clarissa's mouth she let her tongue slide across her lips, wetting them, and then answered. "You."

"Why?"

"Why? What a funny question, my love." AJ

scooped Clarissa up and carried her to the couch, plopping down with Clarissa firmly ensconced on her lap. Pressing her nose into Clarissa's hair, she took a deep breath and enjoyed the warm scent enveloping her. Feeling a lover's energy, savoring their essence and being in tune with them gave AJ a feeling of contentment, and she wasn't about to rush her time with Clarissa. AJ constantly lived with the fear of losing Clarissa niggling in the back of her mind. She would never be settled until De Marcus was dead. Everything else she could handle.

"Maybe—"

AJ put her finger on Clarissa's lips. "I think about you all the time. I watch you sleep and wonder how I find myself lying next to the one person in this world I never thought I would see again. I marvel at the way you've adapted to this world we find ourselves living in now. I know so many of our kind who've slid into degradation, depravity and self-loathing. They medicate themselves, they recreate themselves by turning the most depraved of human kind into vampires, and they've traded what was left of their humanity for hatred of everything breathing. We're faced with a problem that the coven wants to neither address nor take credit for. They've allowed masters to feed wantonly, turning whomever they want and killing those that fight back." AJ pulled Clarissa tighter. "We must be diligent in our lives. We can't become like those who have little regard for life. I've finally found you and I refuse to walk back on the dark side, never again. I won't let us devolve, I won't." AJ buried her nose in to Clarissa's hair and memorized her scent.

"It's a scary place to be right now, isn't it?"

Clarissa burrowed further into AJ's protective embrace.

"Don't be scared. I worry enough for the both of us. You…" AJ turned Clarissa to meet her gaze. "You need to think about finals, grades, and the approaching summer. I think a vacation is in order, don't you?"

"Where did you have in mind?" Clarissa let out an audible sigh. Relinquishing control was never her strong suit, but AJ knew that Clarissa would if asked. All AJ had to do was ask. She didn't want Clarissa to lose the independence she had worked so hard to develop, but she wanted to protect her with every fiber of her being. So, AJ walked the tightrope of protector, but not too protective. She would be whatever Clarissa wanted - lover, champion, or she would step back just enough to give Clarissa the space she needed to feel independent of AJ and her new world. A plant didn't grow if you pulled it up constantly, checking to see if its roots were growing. AJ wanted Clarissa to flower, to grow where she was planted.

"Tuscany?"

"Paris?"

"Really?" AJ was surprised by the suggestion.

"I haven't been back since my family was…" Clarissa swallowed hard and buried her head against AJ.

"It's okay," AJ said, pulling Clarissa tighter.

AJ gently stroked Clarissa's back. She wished she could take Clarissa's pain and carry it for her. AJ's life had never and would never be as harsh as what Clarissa had endured.

"I love you."

"I love you, too," AJ kissed the side of her head and rolled Clarissa on to the couch, their bodies tightly wound together. "You're my world now. I can't imagine my life without you in it. Please never make me find out if I can live without you."

AJ's moment of weakness pulled at Clarissa's heart. It wasn't often that her strong, proud lover confessed her fears. She didn't think she could live life without AJ in it but *she* wasn't as vocal. She knew she still kept her feelings close to her vest, but De Marcus had taught her not to show weakness, ever. A beating stayed with a person longer than a stroke of kindness, and Clarissa had to endure a lifetime's worth of torture at De Marcus' hand. She worked every day to push herself closer to AJ, to open herself to AJ's loving touch, sometimes only to find herself craving the needed caress.

"Careful, you might crush me under the weight of all this mushiness." Clarissa tried to make light of the moment.

"Hmm, am I too heavy?" AJ rolled to her side and snuggled closer on the couch.

"No, I was only kidding. I like the feel of you close to me," Clarissa said, pushing a strand of hair out of AJ's eyes. Her fingertips glided over the planes of AJ's face, her thumb rubbing against her bottom lip. AJ snapped at it, pulling her thumb between her teeth and licking the tip. The sensation sent a jolt through Clarissa before she could pull it back. Trapped, AJ continued to suckle on the tip, eliciting what Clarissa was sure was the desired response. Closing her eyes, she drifted with her lover.

Chapter Three

The coven was a mess. Instead of creating a path Selene could follow, their outdated mindset and ways created roadblocks that she would either have to break down or work around. Selene knew AJ would say bulldoze down the roadblocks and to hell with the coven. Getting De Marcus was the only objective, period.

Flipping through the yellow legal pad she kept on her desk, she studied a few notes and scratched off her last kill. Selene picked up her cell phone and fingered a few numbers.

"He's dead," she said. "You should be getting a package…" Selene pulled the pocket watch from her vest and continued, "Any time now. Transfer the rest of the money, now."

The wise cracking voice on the other end made her want to strangle the bastard, but until he paid, she'd wait. Selene narrowed her eyes as if the person on the other end of the line could see her. After that last snide comment, she'd made up her mind. He was a dead man.

"Later."

The antique watch still lay open in her palm. She ran her finger over the inscription for the thousandth time. She'd had the text re-inscribed several times after wearing it down through years of rubbing. Her mother's words of love to her father knifed through her heart each time she read them. It was the only thing she had of her father and she treasured it more with each passing decade. Opening the other side, she gazed down at the painted face of her mother. She was beautiful and Selene never touched the portrait, fearful her touch would destroy the image and she would be lost to Selene forever. She was in the process of having a large painting made of the image, so she could see her mother every day without worry. Gently closing the watch, she slipped it into the safety of her vest pocket and picked up the phone to call the coven.

After scribbling some notes on the pad, she checked off her client's name and moved to her next item on the to-do list. Gaylord was going to be an exercise in patience. Selene wondered if she could handle talking to the pompous ass.

"Gaylord, please," Selene said, studying her notes.

"Are you requesting to speak to the High Lord of the Eastern Coven?"

"Are you serious?" Leaning back against her chair, she pulled her long dark braid from behind her and flipped it over the seat. Perhaps it was time for a haircut and a change? No, she didn't do changes like that. She was who she was, for now.

"I wouldn't kid about the High Lord. For future reference, please refer to him as High Lord of the Eastern Coven, Gaylord Van der Plume." The nasally voice demanded.

Selene rolled her eyes.

"Geeze, what a pompous ass." A few more words were spat through the phone at Selene. Pulling it away from her ear, she yelled back, "I would like to speak to…oh fine. I'd like to speak to the High Lord of the

Eastern Coven, Gaylord Van der Plume." She listened. "What do you mean I need to make an appointment?"

The voice on the other end gave her instructions to follow and then waited for Selene's reply.

"Fine, when is the *High Lord* available?" Scribbling frantically, Selene drove the tip of the pen through several sheets of paper in frustration. "Tuesday at nine p.m. is fine. Yes, I know how to get there."

She didn't wait for the niceties of ending the conversation, slamming her cell phone closed. No, he couldn't be like anyone else and conduct business over the phone. The way they clung to the antiquated ideas of old was infuriating. Now she would have to trek to the coven for a meeting with Gaylord Van der Plume. She knew why he insisted on a face-to-face. He wanted to exert some control over her but he was in for a big surprise. She wasn't the old Selene.

❧❧❧❧

Rolling her eyes, she wished the bastard were standing close enough that she could choke the dead out of him.

"Fuck. Really, Gaylord? Why do you make me go through all that pomp and circumstance bullshit every fucking time? Asshole."

"Ah, Selene. To what do I owe this pleasure? It's been so long, you rarely are seen at the coven lately."

"Well, I'm not feeling a real connection to the old ways. Besides, you guys aren't that relevant anymore."

"Perhaps not to you, but since you've left we've grown. Expanded into Central American, South America, and well, Africa's been very good to us, too."

"Good for you, Gaylord. I want to talk to you about De Marcus."

"Butch."

"What?"

"I hate Gaylord. Call me Butch."

"Seriously, *Butch*?"

"Much better, now where were we? What happened to you Selene? You were one of us." Butch stood and walked around the massive brocade wingback. His fingers caressed it as one did a lover. "When you killed your master you came to us and became a part of the coven. *We* became your family." He stood resting his elbows along the back of the chair.

"That was a long time ago, Gaylord." He flinched at her use of his given name. She did it to piss him off. Selene wanted him to remember she'd known him a long time and trying to lord over her wasn't going to settle well.

"The coven is still here for you."

"Maybe, but I'm not here for the coven." Her steely gaze pierced Butch's own cold metallic stare. "The coven is old school but times change and so should the teachings. You've lost the ability to move forward with the changing times."

"No one complains about the Catholic Church and its old, stalwart teaching."

"Technology has forced change. The church suffers from its lack of change, it's gushing parishioners. I can't believe you, of all people, are sitting here preaching to me of the church's virtues. You clearly have lost your mind, Gaylord."

"Selene, Selene, Selene," he said, tapping the chair for emphasis. "Come back to the coven. We are stronger than ever. We've added to our numbers, branched out. We've strengthened the covens overseas and have moved forward."

"You said that before." She pointed out the obvious.

He wasn't deterred, as he slung his short frame back into the chair and continued, "We can use more strong, determined women with your skills."

Selene knew what he was implying. Few who still lived in the coven could walk in the daylight. Their old ways kept them firmly rooted in the darkness. Evil always sought out evil. It thrived on the chaos, the power and the weakness of others. To go to the coven would mean giving up the freedom, strength and the light. She wasn't going backwards.

"Thanks, but I'd like to keep my options open. You'll be the first to know if I change my mind," she said sharply. "Now, can we get to the reason I'm here?"

"Of course."

"I want De Marcus."

"You know we are very unhappy with your chosen profession."

"I didn't come here for your blessing. I came here to finish a job. I want De Marcus."

The coven had sent Selene a message a very long time ago voicing their disapproval that Selene had chosen to be nothing more than a glorified hit man. She sloughed it off and continued to do what she was good at, killing people. More importantly her clientele, often vampires themselves, were the ones dictating that vampires were the object of their disdain. The occupation had few perks, but one of them was that people cut her a wide berth, which she rather enjoyed.

"I don't know where he is right now."

"Look, Gaylord, don't wordsmith this shit. You

shouldn't be trying to protect an asshole like that. You just might find yourself going down with him."

"Is that a threat, Selene? Because if it is, the coven has deeper pockets and more people on the payroll than you have time to defend against." Butch suddenly looked pissed. His jovial demeanor was replaced with an all-business attitude.

Selene didn't frighten easy and he should know that. She could push back just as much as he could, only she didn't have to answer to anyone. The coven had strict rules about killing another vampire and he was limited in what he could and couldn't do as far as she was concerned. It surprised her that the coven, more importantly Butch, was protecting De Marcus. De Marcus was a vampire trying to build an empire, and that was in direct conflict with the coven. Worse, he was trolling the bottom of the barrel in his recruitment efforts, and add to that the fact that he tried to kill AJ and Clarissa, should be unforgiveable.

"I'm not threatening Gaylord, I'm stating a fact.

Chapter Four

AJ worried the pencil she was biting. De Marcus was starting to concern her—better said, he was still loose and a problem. Clarissa's life was at risk and she worked every day to keep Clarissa safe. She'd rewired her penthouse suite with cameras that captured every movement down to a mouse flicking its whiskers. The motion sensors were sensitive enough to catch the slightest draft wafting the drapes and her staff was on constant alert for any possible breach in security.

"Hey baby." Clarissa wrapped her arms around AJ's neck and nuzzled her. "You work too much." She twisted the chair around and planted herself in AJ's lap.

"Do I now?"

"Hmm, you do, my love."

The throbbing in Clarissa's neck was like a beacon calling to AJ's lost ship. A quick flick of her incisors and she would be on a collision path with her lover. They entwined, her lips pulling on Clarissa's neck as she sucked. Her heart thumped loud enough that she knew Clarissa could hear her intent.

"Yes, I do know what you're thinking, Sweetheart." Clarissa slid her tongue across AJ's full lips. "I've known what you're thinking all night. I'm surprised I had to come to you. Are you avoiding me?"

"Avoiding you?"

"Well." Clarissa, popped a button, then closed her eyes and inhaled. "You've been preoccupied and…" Another button popped off AJ's shirt and skittered across the floor. "I've been sending you signals all night," Clarissa said, ripping AJ's shirt open.

"Aw, that was my favorite shirt." AJ stood and lifted her up, wrapping Clarissa's legs around her waist.

"I didn't know you had a favorite shirt."

"I don't but—"

Clarissa pressed her lips against AJ's. Warm, wet tongues dueled for position as AJ slipped her hand behind Clarissa and released the snaps on her bra. Pulling her hips closer, AJ reached around front with her other hand and tweaked a nipple. A squeal and Clarissa was loose and running for the bedroom.

The chase was on.

"You can run, my love…" AJ sprinted around the bed. She caught Clarissa by the waist and pulled her down on top of her. Flipping Clarissa onto her back, she straddled her hips and positioned herself over her lover. As they locked their gaze, AJ ached for her. She felt it in her bones, her heart clenched and she couldn't stop herself. Piercing the soft skin of Clarissa's neck, she lowered down and licked the trickle of blood that oozed out. The tingle that shot through her landed solidly on her clit. Her hips begged for hard contact as she bucked against Clarissa. It was all she could do not to return the favor and rip Clarissa's clothing to shreds. Divesting herself of her ripped blouse she pushed Clarissa's up and craned her neck for a taste of the dark, pebbled areolas. AJ moved from one breast to the other, flicking the tips and suckling each one before Clarissa pushed her lower. She nipped the soft skin of Clarissa's tight, flinching stomach as she worked her way farther down.

Clarissa pleaded for the kind of relief only AJ could provide. AJ lifted her hips and tossed slacks and panties to the floor. Standing, she looked down, admiring Clarissa's innocent beauty. She glowed, still looking like the inexperienced lover AJ had known so many decades earlier. Outstretched hands beckoned AJ to join her on the bed, and she couldn't resist the offer.

"You're so bad, my love."

"Am I? In what way?" AJ smiled, slipping her clothes off and snuggling next to Clarissa.

Clarissa guided AJ's hand between her legs. Flattening AJ's palm against her, she slid a finger into her wetness. She was practically purring as AJ started to work Clarissa's opening wider. Two fingers paused just at the entrance, before Clarissa pushed them inside. A groan followed a flood of wetness that coated AJ's hand.

"You make me wait for you. I haven't learned patience in all these many years," Clarissa said, grinding against AJ's hand. "I don't want to wait to be together ever again. Promise me you'll…"

The sensation of a flush spreading through Clarissa made AJ surge with heat. Every sensation, every touch, every nuanced emotion worked its way through both of their bodies, heightening AJ's already hypersensitive awareness. The tremor before the rush of Clarissa's orgasm made AJ's body jerk at the same time. Slipping her tongue into Clarissa's mouth, she pushed deeper. Urgency replaced patience, need replaced want.

A sliver of light sliced across their bodies. Running her finger through it, Clarissa marveled at the fact she could even do so without pain. She'd been a light walker for decades. She didn't remember exactly when it happened, but she suspected gradually. She'd played a game of hide and seek with the sunlight for a century. In the past, she'd push her hand into the shade and pull it back, eventually noticing that the warmth during the day didn't affect her. A hand, then an arm, and finally her whole body embraced the opportunity to be whole again. Sunglasses allowed her to sit in the warmth of the light. Who knew there was *warm* shade as Clarissa referred to the half sun, half shade, but there it was, Darwin's theory in action. *The survival of the fittest adapted with time.* While her eyes had a tougher time, eventually they'd adjusted, too.

Clarissa let her finger follow the sliver of light along her lover's body, across her tight ass, down a thigh and off. Her tongue dipped into the light as she traced it.

"Oh, you're ready for more?" AJ turned over and pulled Clarissa on top of her.

Resting her chin on her fists, Clarissa could only smile as her gaze met AJ's. Her hair fanned out across the pillow in odd directions and the rosy blush colored her pale cheeks.

"Do you think we'll ever tan?"

AJ's brow furrowed. Staring at the lips that had quirked up at the question, Clarissa let her finger trace the shallow bow of AJ's top lip. Before she could say anything, AJ had snapped her lips around the finger and started to suck on it.

"I see you're not in the mood for pillow talk."

Clarissa squirmed as the suction sent a jolt through her.

Pulling her finger back, she placed her hands on each side of AJ's head and tried to lift herself up. AJ took control, rolling her quickly onto her back.

"I'm not in the mood for pillow talk." AJ straddled Clarissa and pressed her hands above her head. With Clarissa trapped, she attacked her neck again. The loss of control sent Clarissa reeling and anxiety pierced her body. Her fight or flight response asserted control of her mind. She bucked her hips against AJ.

"Stop."

AJ popped her head up with a confused look. "Seriously?"

"Yes." Clarissa tried to wiggle out of AJ's grasp. "Please, get off." Panic laced her voice. She knew AJ could feel it.

Easy, my love, I was just responding in kind to your touch.

I'm sorry, I was feeling trapped. I could feel my throat tighten, and my body...

Clarissa's body shook uncontrollably, forcing her to curl into herself.

Baby, what's wrong. What did I do?

AJ wrapped her in a protective embrace. She sensed AJ's concern for her instantly, but that couldn't neutralize the fear inside. A flashback suddenly overtook her.

"Control it, Clarissa. I said control it, damn it." *De Marcus swung the leather strap over her back.*

The sting of the leather bit into her back as she lay naked on the floor of the cottage. Her body was betraying her mind. Another bite of the leather across her back and she felt her incisors lengthen.

"I said control it, you bitch," he yelled, as he swung again.

Clarissa cursed him under her breath. He watched as another vampire brought her to orgasm again, only to beat it out of her. She panted as she tried to focus on something other than the betrayal of her body. Another tingle shot through her body and then the strap hit her again.

"If you don't learn to respond only to me, you will be at anyone's beck and call." He whipped her again.

"Fuck you." She spat blood at him.

"Oh I will, but not before you learn your lesson, my love. Trust me, this hurts me more than it will hurt you if this happens again." He swung the leather strap across her back once more.

"De Marcus, must we—" the man pleaded in earnest.

"Shut the fuck up. She needs to learn that I am her master and only me."

"Fine, but I am done with this folly. She has learned her lesson, I'm sure. Don't call me again, if this is what you want next time." Reaching down, the man caressed Clarissa's shoulder and said, "I'm sorry, Clarissa. Please forgive me."

With that, the lesson was over. Clarissa lay on the floor for quite some time as De Marcus smoked a cigar and preached to her the virtues of self-control.

"He did that to you? I'm going to kill that bastard. Why would you remember that, did I hurt you tonight? Did I do something you didn't like? I'm confused." The hurt in AJ's voice broke Clarissa's heart.

"I can't seem to control the flashbacks, AJ" Clarissa started to silently weep.

She'd been having more of them recently and she couldn't figure out why. Nothing had changed in her life. She was happier than ever. She'd found out the love of her life hadn't killed her family as she once suspected. They were together and blissfully happy. Something had happened and she couldn't put her finger on what it was, so she struggled with the flashbacks.

"Perhaps you should see someone?"

"Who? Who is safe enough to spill all my secrets too? I'm a vampire who's lived for over a century. That's bound raise some eyebrows don't you think?"

"Me, then. You can talk to me," AJ offered.

Turning to face AJ, she cupped her face and smiled weakly. She didn't have to say anything. AJ would sense it, feel it, see it in her mind's eye if she wanted too. She hoped AJ would stay out of her thoughts, but it was inevitable they shared everything.

"I think I need some time."

"Meaning?"

"I need some space to try and figure this out. Something's happened, something's upside down in my world…" Clarissa put her finger over AJ's lips, stopping her before she could say anything. "It's not you. Trust me, you're the best thing that's happened to me in a very long time. I'm going to stay at my place for a while. I think it will help me. You're too close. Our thoughts merge all the time. You see what I'm thinking and sometimes I don't want you to know what De Marcus did to me. I don't want to remember what De Marcus did to me, but it's happening."

"But—"

"No buts, I've decided. After we have dinner with Selene, I'm going home for a little while. It's not forever, just for a while. Besides, you need space, too. You don't run anymore, you don't ride your motorcycle; you've been so wrapped up in 'us' that you've lost all sense of who AJ is."

"I like where my life is. I love being with you." AJ pulled Clarissa's hand to her lips and softly laid a kiss on her knuckles, then turned it over and kissed her palm. "De Marcus is out there and he's not going to stop hunting for you or me. He's determined to kill us."

Trying to make light of the comment, Clarissa responded, "Maybe if we split up we'll be harder to kill. If we're together, it makes it easier for him to get us both."

Clarissa knew she was safest with AJ, but her need to be alone was suddenly more than she could explain.

"I worry."

"I know, but don't. I'm not the same woman as I was even months ago. I'll be careful. I'll call every day. I'll talk to you so much you'll beg me to quit bugging you." Clarissa tried to give a reassuring smile, but it was weak at best.

"I doubt it."

"I need to do this, honey, and I need you to understand."

"I might understand, but I won't like it."

"I know my love, I know." Clarissa felt a little more than sad as she held AJ tighter. She hoped she was doing the right thing. Facing the problem on her own was the only way to figure out what was happening to her.

Chapter Five

Selene rolled down her cuffs and buttoned them. Her new tattoo was to celebrate—no, remind her of the job she'd completed. The artwork today added to the small sleeve tribute to her family. She was the only survivor of a brutal attack that had turned her into an animal, and knew she wasn't far from that very animal today. The only difference now was that she could control it better. Selene flashed back to that fateful night. In an instant, she met the new world she would either have to embrace or run from for an eternity.

They had barely finished the modest home they lived in when a traveler came by one night and asked her father for lodging. He had offered their barn to the dashing young man, telling him that with a house full of women, it was the best he could offer.

The urge to meet a possible husband had sent her sisters aflame, something Selene couldn't understand. Her two sisters had put together a basket, thinking the traveler might be hungry and, of course, it gave them the perfect excuse to visit. They had gathered their courage and asked her, as the elder sister, to be the lookout. Selene watched as her sisters went to the barn. Sneaking behind them, she sat in the shadows outside and watched as her sisters flirted with the traveler. After sitting for a few minutes, the young man pounced on her sisters, ripping them to shreds. Selene remembered screaming as she ran for the house. Before she had taken only a few steps, he was standing over her covered in blood. His gaze kept her transfixed, unable to move, or to warn her parents. Picking her up, he remarked how lucky he had been to find such accommodating lodging with a meal plan. The last thing she remembered as he bit her was the sound of a shotgun firing.

Selene woke to find herself lying in a pool of her father's blood. His throat had been ripped open. She shuddered looking into eyes staring at nothing. Running into the house, she found her mother lying in blood soaked sheets. A gurgle escaped her lips.

"Run." Was all her mother had the strength to say before she died.

She wiped at the sweat rolling down her face and neck. She had a visceral reaction every time she time-traveled back to her beginnings. Her only compensation was she had killed the man who had taken her family and given her a gift she never wanted. Immortality.

Before she could even knock the door swung wide and AJ stood looking at her.

"So are you just going to stand there all night or are you going to come in…" AJ lowered her head towards Selene and whispered, "and help me eat Clarissa's newest creation."

Without a word of greeting, she walked past AJ and towards certain gastric agony. Clarissa stood hovered over a steaming pot, tossing something in it and mumbling. Sensing her tension, Selene gave AJ a quizzical look.

AJ shrugged and offered a seat. "Sit. Can I get you something to drink?"

"Whiskey neat would be fine. Thank you." Selene

felt more uncomfortable than a new kid at school. She had that feeling she was intruding on a personal moment between AJ and Clarissa. The heat between the two was palpable. "I'm not interrupting anything am I? I can just leave if I am…I mean I don't want to intrude on…" Selene looked at Clarissa and back to AJ "You know."

"You don't need to be so formal, Selene. We are friends," AJ said. "So spit it out."

AJ handed Selene her drink and smiled as if they were sharing a secret. It made her uncomfortable, but then being in AJ's penthouse made her uncomfortable.

"Well this is awkward." Selene sipped her drink hoping it would work faster than AJ's mouth.

"Oh, you think we need to be alone to have sex?"

Selene cleared her throat and sipped again. It was more of a chug, but it had the same burning affect. She shot AJ a look that would have wilted most men, but not AJ. She only laughed and slapped Selene on the back.

"We already did that, buddy," AJ whispered and thankfully didn't expand further on the answer.

So that's what Selene was feeling, that post-colloidal some couples shared after sex. The energy in the room was electric and Selene shivered internally. One of the pitfalls of being a vampire, you could sense things whether you wanted to or not. Selene hadn't had sex in months due to her self-imposed celibacy that kept her head clearer. So the sexual tension was screwing with her overly reactive body. The blood lust from the kill earlier had barely settled in and she was wound tighter than a bundle of barbed wire. She always found a willing sexual partner to work through the blood lust, usually another vampire, because they could handle the immense surge of power that pulsed through her body.

"You okay? You seem tight." AJ rotated her shoulder, the way a football player did when warming up. "Did you have a job, is that why you're so keyed up?"

Selene sat on the leather sofa and ran her hand over the butter-soft surface. She could feel the residual sexual energy pushing off it, so she stood and walked over to the floor-to-ceiling window. The view was spectacular up top.

"I'm fine," was all Selene offered. She wasn't a chatty kind of person, especially after a kill, and then there was her trip to the coven. The bad news she had to deliver to AJ wouldn't be easy, but she suspected AJ knew what the coven would say, so perhaps it wouldn't matter one way or the other. She was still going to kill De Marcus with or without Selene.

"Hey, there you are. I didn't hear you come in. Guess I was busy trying to make sure everything is perfect." Clarissa threaded her arm around Selene and reached up to place a kiss on her cheek. "So, how have you been? We haven't see much of you lately, you okay?"

Clarissa pulled Selene's face closer, trying to catch her gaze. Selene looked down into a face that hadn't aged in a century. Clarissa still appeared all of twenty, maybe twenty-one years old. It was amazing how time, experiences, and the death of your family couldn't put a wrinkle on a face. Selene and Clarissa had similar backgrounds, their families were murdered when they were young and they survived in spite of the loss. However, one was still as innocent as the driven snow and the other was dark and murderous.

"I've been busy. Sorry. I should make it a point to see you more now that I know where you live." Selene smiled at her weak joke.

"Yes, and you shouldn't let that big meanie over there keep you away." Clarissa pointed at AJ who feigned being crushed by the innuendo. The glance the two exchanged warmed Selene's heart. She often wished she could find someone like Clarissa, to equal out her life, bring her some semblance of joy.

"She doesn't. I've really just been busy."

"Well, I hope you're hungry. Have you acquired a taste for certain foods? I find that I do better with a more bland diet. British food serves me best."

"I'm not sure. I pop these little babies." Selene pulled her tin and shook it. The pills echoed in the container. "Eating is such a chore, don't you think?" She suddenly regretted her comment. "I'm sorry, I didn't mean to say that. I just meant that I have better things to do…I mean…I don't have time to…Shit."

Clarissa just smiled at the way Selene tried to wordsmith her way out of the verbal blunder, but she was sure she'd insulted Clarissa without meaning too.

"It's all right. If you eat, great, if you don't it's still great to see you." Clarissa returned to the kitchen, but not before informing them that dinner was ready. "Wash your hands before you sit down."

"Is she serious?" Selene suddenly felt like a kid.

"Afraid so, buddy. Bathroom's right down the hall," AJ said, pointing to the last door.

This is going to be a long night, fuck. Selene ran her hands under the water, squirted some soap on them and rinsed again. No one had mothered her in decades, funny how she rebelled against it even now. Wiping her hands on the soft, fluffy towel she marveled at the way her place was so different than AJ's home. It *was* a home wasn't it? Clarissa had added little elements, and if one knew AJ, would never believe how cozy it was now. The soft towels, the black and white photographs on the walls, the aroma of a home cooked meal wafting through the house. Definitely not signs of vampire living. Pulling the tin from her pocket, she opened it and took a capsule. Before she could break it, she heard Clarissa calling her name. Pop an enhanced blood substitute or eat a meal. Staring at the dark red horse pill, she put it back in the tin and groaned. It would be in bad taste not to eat Clarissa's food. Like it or not she would eat, compliment the cook and wish she hadn't indulged.

"So, you went to the coven?" AJ asked. "What did Van Der Plume have to say? Is he going to help us?"

"Honey, it's dinner time, you can talk business later."

Clarissa placed a few boiled potatoes on Selene's plate along with a sliced sausage and some over-cooked vegetables. Selene sighed and picked up her fork and knife and speared a potato. She hadn't had silverware in her hands, at least to eat, in years. A coffee, a cookie, a drink – all small, easy to handle and didn't take up much space or require intensive digestive energy. But she knew more vampires were eating. She could taste it in their blood on the few occasions she had indulged her old habits. While rare, she often found one of her clients – kills – was a vampire and so she indulged. The high one got when feeding off another vampire was explosive.

Focusing back on her plate, she pushed the food around before spearing the slick potato. Slicing it in half, she picked it up and inspected it from all angles before popping it in her mouth. She moved her tongue around it, over it and finally bit it. The texture was exactly as she remembered it. Soft, and warm, she could taste a hint of the dirt it had been grown in. Chewing it repeatedly until it was mush, she took a swig of her drink to help wash it down.

Peering up she noticed both AJ and Clarissa were staring at her obviously waiting for a reaction.

"So?"

"It's fine."

"You sure?" AJ inquired before starting on her own small plate.

"I'm sure." Selene motioned toward their plates. "Eat."

Selene hadn't been around a lot of her kind that were able to eat, so watching AJ and Clarissa push their food around and then finally take a mouthful was comical. Eating was like being a light walker, it happened gradually. It seemed that some vampire's took to eating like they did turning humans, with great gusto. She'd killed her share of fat bastards, and after biting them she had to spit out the blood, tainted from the crap they ate. Junk food wasn't just for humans, it seemed vamps liked it as well.

"So." AJ pushed back a semi-clean plate.

Selene was surprised that AJ had eaten the bland dinner. Perhaps the lack of flavor was why she could eat. Clarissa snatched the plate off the table and interrupted AJ.

"Would you like more, honey? Selene?"

"I'm good. Thanks, Clarissa. I'm watching my weight. I wouldn't want to pack on a few pounds and hurt my ability to work."

"Hmm. You look like you need a cookie, Selene, or a whole pack. You really should consider eating more. With your metabolism I would think you could burn 'em off in an hour. How about you, honey?"

"I'll take a plate later, beautiful. Save one of those sausages. They were good," AJ sighed. "So, back to the coven, what did they say about helping us with De Marcus?"

"Butch—"

"Who is Butch?"

"Gaylord wants to be called, Butch." Selene said, turning her chair around and stretching her legs out.

"Jesus, guess he wants to change with the times." AJ shook her head. "So what did he say?"

Selene fidgeted with the cuff of her shirt. Her tattoo itched, but she didn't want to scratch it and screw-up the ink. She was sure it was almost healed, vampires healed almost too quickly. AJ cleared her throat, making Selene look up.

"Well?"

Selene shook her head. "He can't help."

"Can't or won't?"

"Is there a difference? He says he doesn't know where De Marcus is—"

"Bullshit." AJ slammed her fist on the table. "He's protecting the bastard."

"I have no doubt. Butch knows exactly where he's at, or what he's involved in. I'm thinking the coven is protecting him for a reason."

"Why? He's violated every tenant they hold up as law to the rest of the coven and yet they let *him* live. Why?"

"I told Butch to be careful, he could find himself going down with De Marcus."

"You threatened the High Lord? I bet he didn't appreciate that."

"Look, this was just a job at first. That changed when I found out De Marcus was after Clarissa, but *Butch* is making it personal. I think he's trying to get me to come back into the coven. Said as much in our conversation. He said the coven is extending its reach. He claims they're deep in East Asia, Eastern Europe and Africa. They don't seem to mind that some masters are even turning druggies and gang-bangers. As long as they're fighting amongst themselves he doesn't care. A family is a family."

Selene stood and walked back over to the window, staring down at the people walking in the waning light of the sun. If they only knew what was waiting around the corner for some of them. The towering apartments hugging the sprawling park were like cement crypts. Only they lived in these, but soon for some of them, they would be just that, their crypts.

"I'm going to the coven and talk to *Butch*. The bastard owes me an explanation. De Marcus tried to kill me and Clarissa, and I'm not going to allow them to hide him. They can offer him up willingly or they can pay the price. I don't care."

"I wouldn't do that."

"Why? They don't own me. I've paid my debt long ago. My master is dead. I'm free to do what I want, Selene."

"Look, he made it clear that he has more resources, and could make our lives miserable."

"Big talk for an asshole who hasn't seen daylight in centuries."

"I wouldn't underestimate him, AJ. He wasn't kidding when he said he would take out a mark on us."

"I'm surprised, Selene. It sounds like you're afraid."

Selene wasn't afraid, just cautious. She didn't overplay her hand and she definitely didn't make empty threats. Unlike AJ, she rarely let emotion set her pace. A slow, methodically thought out plan would bring De Marcus to her. She wouldn't chase the bastard, but wait and bait a trap he couldn't resist.

"Calm down—"

"Don't fucking tell me to call down." AJ grabbed Selene's shirt and pulled her closer. Both women dropped fangs and growled. "We're talking about Clarissa here and if anything happens to her, god help those who hurt her…or couldn't protect her."

Selene grabbed AJ's hands, her extended fingernails digging into her flesh. The smell of blood was instantaneous, sending a thrill through Selene.

"Hey, what the hell are you two doing?" Clarissa said, trying to step between the two vampires. Selene was pushed back away from AJ. *Lucky for her.* Selene felt blood lust take over. Anger and blood where a bad mix and often led to death, or at a slim minimum, a badly damaged vamp. AJ's hand still firmly gripped her shirt when Selene heard it.

Rrrriiiipppppp.

"AJ!" Shocked, Clarissa turned and pushed AJ back, still clutching the front of Selene's shirt.

"Selene?"

Each woman was locked on the other, both waiting for an excuse to attack. Selene could see in her peripheral vision, the tatters of her black button down barely covering her naked breasts. She broke in a sweat as she tried to control changing from her human form. Her gut ached as she held on to the last fragments of her human instinct.

"AJ, let her go. Now!"

"Her first," AJ snarled.

If anything she pulled tighter on what was left of Selene's shirt. Yanking AJ's hand closer, Selene tried to whisper over Clarissa's head. "You don't want a piece of me, let me assure you of that. Now take your hands off me so I can keep what's left of my dignity and go home."

"Oh, oh, no you haven't had dessert yet, Selene. Please don't go." Clarissa turned to AJ and continued, "See what you've done. We haven't seen her in weeks and now she's leaving before we've even had a chance to chat. God, I hate when you women go all butch on each other." Clarissa extricated herself from the mass of arms and stomped into the kitchen, cussing.

"You girlfriend is pissed." Selene's smirk signaled a check in her win column.

"She'll get over it, trust me," AJ said, undeterred by Clarissa's anger.

"Aren't you barking up the wrong tree? I'm not the one you have a beef with. You should be taking this up with De Marcus."

"I plan on it." AJ pushed Selene backwards. "I'm going to the coven to see Butch and have it out with him. I'm not going to stand for this bullshit. The coven is an antiquated machine that needs to be dismantled."

"And you think you're going to do that when you visit him? Trust me, he isn't going to take threats lightly. If anything you'll only make him dig his heels in more."

"I don't care." AJ poured herself a whiskey and sat. "I've had it with them. They let these two-bit hoods turn humans for their own perverted self-interest. They pick the slime up out of the bottom of the barrel — gangsters, thugs, and drug addicts, people who already have deep seeded issues with authority and make them super human. Turning them loose on the world to do their bidding, and we're supposed to sit back keep our mouth shut and watch? I don't think so. Eventually, the humans are going to get wise to what's going on and put together a covert extermination plan. We won't know about it until it's too late. If they're tapping into our cell phones, emails and god knows what else, you can bet they know who and where we are and I don't like that. I'm considering going underground for a while. I've got stuff stashed for a long hibernation and if this shit goes south, we're gone. If you wanna come along let me know. I stocked up for a long winter, if you know what I mean.

AJ's erratic mental state was a concern to Selene. She was normally pretty even keeled, but when she was under a lot of stress, she'd seen AJ take down men with one blow. She sorta pitied Butch; he had no idea what he was in for. AJ could make it an all-out war with very few survivors. All she wanted was De Marcus and now Selene had to wonder why Butch was working so hard to hide him.

"Don't say I didn't warn you if you do decide to go to the coven. I'd make an appointment, first. Seems Butch doesn't like surprises."

"Really?" AJ sipped her whiskey then purred. "Well then we'll just have to surprise him won't we?"

This was not going to end well.

Chapter Six

Selene stalked though the full parking lot at the Dungeon. Maggie, her business partner, would be thrilled to see so many patrons, but after a night of verbal jousting with AJ, her mood soured quickly. Even Clarissa's gentle joking couldn't pull Selene through the night. What was it about her darn cat Nefertiti? The damn thing lay sprawled across her lap half the night. Each time she pushed it off, she found the persistent feline comfortably ensconced on her lap. Finally, she gave up and just let it stay. The cat hair covered her pressed black slacks and cashmere sweater she'd manage to put on after AJ's little outburst and tantrum that cost her a perfectly good button-down.

She wasn't an animal lover at all. In fact, she considered them an appetizer on those rare moments when she craved a liquid diet. A guilty pleasure for sure.

Entering the club, her vision sharpened instantly allowing her to see everything. The noise on the other hand was almost non-existent. She focused her hearing and could only hear the occasional gasp. The smell of women in estrus slammed against her, almost making her turn around and leave. Her body was buffeted by the sensation and it was all Selene could do to stay in control. Taking long deep breaths, she inhaled the sexual frenzy and looked around the room at the packed jars of estrogen filling the seats. Jax must be doing another demo night for the ladies. Ever since those trashy books, what were they named? Selene tried to remember. Oh, it didn't matter, but ever since those "mommy porn" books came out she couldn't turn the women away. She wasn't complaining, it had been good for business without having to lift a finger in advertising, a boon to her pocket book and her sex life if she were honest.

Jax rested his elbows on the bar, clearly engaged by the scene unfolding on stage. He was like a vulture waiting for the show to be over so he could have his pick of horny, over-stimulated women eager to experiment. The tension of the room raised a level, each body generating its own wave of energy that pelted Selene. Sliding her hand against the rough texture of the wooden bar, she turned and watched the show. Too much salt in tonight's dinner made Selene's mouth feel like a wad of cotton. Luckily she had eaten sparingly. Her system just wasn't ready for a full on meal. The sunlight had taken time and so would food.

Snapping her fingers next to Jax's ear she tried to get his attention.

"Jax."

No response, and she focused once again on the stage show.

Mistress Rose had a way of pulling her audience into her web of kink. Once there, they rarely realized until it was too late that they were often doing something they normally wouldn't be caught dead doing. Add a little alcohol and most people became like putty in her well-manicured hands. *What happens in the club, stays in the club*, she told every audience.

Little did they know that every face, every action was caught on tape somewhere in the club. Mostly for insurance purposes, but once or twice Selene had been thankful she'd had the tapes when the cops had arrived claiming a rape had taken place.

Mistress Rose strutted across the stage to the "volunteer" who was usually one of the Dungeon staffers. The audience sat enraptured by the precise display of whipmanship Mistress Rose commanded. Selene was often surprised Rose managed to stay tucked into her tightly laced leather corset. Her supple breasts with just a hint of nipple showing begged for release, but they would stay safely tucked for the remainder of the show, Selene was sure.

Mistress Rose spotted Selene at the bar, and winked then licked her ruby tinted lips. It was game on now for Rose. Selene had been able to keep her advances at bay, but it seemed anytime she spotted Selene near, she upped the ante. Suddenly, Selene felt sorry for the volunteer. She would be the recipient of the torture Rose wanted to share with Selene. She would have to try and prevent it the only way she knew how. She turned her back on the action and ignored the Mistress' gestures that were a ploy to get Selene to respond.

"Jax." She snapped her fingers near his ear again. "Two fingers of Jack."

"You got it, Boss."

The crack of the whip exploded throughout the club and the audience gasped.

"She's hot for ya boss," Jax said, pushing her drink towards her and nodding his head at the stage.

"Yeah, well the feeling isn't mutual."

Selene swallowed the liquid in one gulp, a slow

burn her reward. Slamming her glass down, she ordered another.

She could smell someone coming up on her before movement out of the corner of her eye caught her attention. A glance in the mirror behind the bar found her staring at a platinum blonde as she tried to catch Jax's attention.

"Excuse me," she whispered.

"What can I getcha?" Jax said, finishing his generous pour in Selene's glass.

"Rum and coke, two beers in bottles, a strawberry daiquiri and margarita—on the rocks," she said, clicking them off her fingers.

"Coming right up."

The woman seemed out of place. Not exactly the mommy type, with kids at home. Locking eyes with her in the mirror, Selene quirked a smile, taking a slow, deep breath, *estrus*. She glanced away, not waiting to stare and then looked at Rose behind her. The mirror gave her the opportunity to keep an eye on the whole club and not look like a creeper: Selene's definition for men who came in to scout out women during ladies night. The creep trolled the room, trying to pick-up anything with tits and too much alcohol.

Jax slid the drinks towards the woman and took her cash. She looked bewildered, trying to figure out how to get so many drinks to the table of screaming women.

"Here let me help you with those," Jax said, seeing a *creeper* opportunity.

"I'll get 'em. You stay behind the bar." Selene grabbed three of the drinks before the woman had a chance to reject her help.

"Oh, you don't have to do that, I can come back

and get the rest." A slight blush colored her pale skin. Skin that obviously hadn't been kissed by the sun in years, if ever. Selene didn't pick-up anything earlier when she scanned the club, so she wasn't one of hers.

"Thank you, that's very kind of you."

"Just doing my job." Selene smiled.

"I wouldn't want to be any trouble." the woman said, trying not to make eye contact.

Selene could feel the woman's pulse quicken, her body shooting off pheromones and a rush of blood colored her checks.

"It's no trouble, I assure you miss…"

"Oh, Francesca, but my friends call me Francesca." Another blush.

"Well Francesca, if I can be of further service." Selene sat the drinks on the table. "Please let me know."

"Hello, tall dark and gorgeous. Are you part of the entertainment tonight?" One of the women at the table touched Selene's hand. The heat from the woman pelted Selene as she looked down at the slightly plump, sweating woman.

Ignoring the slight, Selene patted the hand and tried to be charming to the paying patrons. "No, I'm the owner. I don't —" She often liked to work the back rooms, opting not to mention it for fear she might find the overzealous woman waiting for her in the back.

"Oh, with those looks and that killer body." The woman stood, and grabbed Selene's biceps. "You work out don'tcha? Girls, check out these arms." She ran her hand down Selene's stomach. "Oh, abs of steel, too."

Selene grabbed the hand, stopping it from going

any further. "Careful, miss. You might bite off more than you can chew."

"Oh god that voice, sexy. You could read the phone book to me and I would swoon."

"Well, if you think you can *handle* me, I give private lessons in the back, if you're interested." Selene leaned down and growled into the woman's ear, loud enough for all at the table to hear.

The woman fell back into her seat as if she'd been blown over and fanned herself.

"Hey, boss?" Jax yelled for her.

"Sorry, ladies, duty calls." Selene nodded at the women. "I hope you enjoy the rest of your evening."

A chorus of *aahhhss* followed her as she weaved her way through the crowded floor.

She could hear the women whisper about private lessons and wanting to play *student* to Selene's *teacher*. Thoughts of the heavy woman in a school girl outfit flashed in Selene's mind and was just as quickly dismissed when the image made her want to gag. The only voice not saying anything was Francesca's, but Selene could feel her eyes watching as she walked to the bar.

"Thank you," Selene said to Jax, appreciative of the *save*.

"No problem," Jax said. "You looked a little uncomfortable. When I saw that woman put her hands on your stomach I thought, 'oh man that chick is going to lose a hand', good self-control, boss."

"She was going to lose more than a hand if she kept pawing me."

Leaning against the bar, Selene watched the stage and then scanned the crowd. Her gaze sought out Francesca's, an apologetic smile seemed to be her reward for the glance. She dipped her head in thanks and lifted her glass towards Francesca. Oddly, she felt Francesca knew exactly what she was thinking. God, what she wouldn't do to give *her* private lessons.

Chapter Seven

The women at the table embarrassed Francesca. How could such highly educated, hardworking researchers act like teenage boys with their first girlie magazine? Only this girlie magazine walked and talked. Well, more like stroked their ears with the low tenor of her voice, but it had the desired affect if that was what she was going for. Their overt ogling of the Dungeon's owner had her mentally apologizing for such crass behavior. The owner was gracious as Dorothy ran her hands over her arms and stomach. The owner advertised her intentions when she whispered in Dorothy's ear, and it had shut the bitch up in an instant. Francesca's mind reeled at the possibilities. What lay behind the back doors of the club? More of what she saw on stage? Coming to the club wasn't exactly her idea. It had started as a dare and ended here tonight. Suddenly, without reason, she was intrigued by the possibilities of anonymity and experimentation.

"Hey girls, check this out," Dorothy said waving *the shiny club card around. "This was on my car this morning."*

The women in the lunchroom bunched around to get a look.

"Ooo, it's for one of those bondage clubs," said *one of the gals as she ran her finger over the muscled man in leather.*

Flipping the card over Dorothy read the writing on the back, "Check this out, free lady's night. They call it—Thirsty Thursdays. Come quench your thirst and feed your appetite for whips, leather and sin. Hmm, sounds fun. Who's in?" Dorothy glanced at the women who were still huddled around the card.

"I wanna go," said one gal.

"Well...okay if you go, Millie, I'll go," a blonde said as she wiggled her eyebrows. "This might be fun. I've never been to a place like that. I'll tell Tim I'm going to a candle party. He won't care."

"How about you Francesca? Wanna go?" Dorothy looked at Francesca and smiled.

"Francesca won't go, she's too practical."

"What? What are you talking about Millie?" Francesca tried to look indignant, but Millie was right, this wasn't Francesca's idea of a good time. Sweat, leather and watching people being tied up and spanked just didn't appeal to her.

"Look, you're predictable. Every Monday for the past three years, you bring tuna on whole wheat, a green apple sliced in six pieces and a diet coke. On Tuesday, you bring a turkey on rye with mustard on the side, because you don't want it to get soggy, cheddar potato chips and a diet coke. On Wednesday you—"

"I get it. Fine, I'm in. Just don't ask me to do anything. Okay?" Francesca instantly regretted her decision. She was not predictable, just practical, there was a difference.

"Ten bucks says, she backs out," someone whispered.

"Okay I'll take that bet, I won't back out. You just make sure you don't, 'kay?"

By Thursday, the women were thoroughly

worked up about their date at the Dungeon—everyone but Francesca. She had tried to think of a way to get out of tonight, but by the time they finished lunch everyone had taken the ten dollar bet and now if anyone backed out they would all owe the others eighty bucks. She would never live down backing out on a bet.

Eighty bucks, how did I let myself be talked into this? Thought Francesca as she changed her clothes.

Amateur night was something the Dungeon did once a month for those that wanted to see what BDSM was like. The women grabbed a table close to the stage and ordered drinks over the erotic beat with too much bass. The darkened room made it difficult to see anything or anyone. Francesca was thankful, although it made no sense, since all of her co-workers were already there.

The lights dimmed even further, if that was possible, and the spotlight hit a tall, slim man dressed in leather.

"Ladies and Gentlemen, welcome to the Dungeon. How many are here for the first time?" He surveyed the darkened room. "Hmm, I see a lot of hands. Well, welcome to your first experience in bondage. If you're squeamish, feel light headed or need assistance, we have people around the room that can help you get some fresh air." Chuckling at his own joke he continued, "It won't be that bad, I promise."

As he walked off the stage, a man strapped to an X was wheeled out, his backside shown to the audience. A woman in a tight leather bustier and stiletto heels, brandishing a whip, came on stage from the other side. Crack, and then another crack rang out as the woman skillfully snapped the whip over the crowd.

"Ooooo," everyone whispered as the audience ducked their heads, afraid they might be accidentally hit by the long menacing whip.

From across the stage, the woman criss-crossed the man's now shimmering back. Each time he asked the woman for another lash.

"One ma'am," he said, until he had counted off thirty strikes.

"Should we give him more ladies?"

"Noooo!" screamed the crowd as the man was wheeled off the stage.

"Well, who's next, then?" She gazed out into the audience. "Perhaps we have volunteers?" She gave the ladies' table a smile and winked. Raising a suggestive eyebrow, she moved to the next table. With no takers for her offer, she waved at the crowd, flashed a final smile and left the stage.

The tall, leather clad gentleman returned to the stage, slapping a short handled flogger against his hand.

"Ladies, are you having fun tonight?" Cupping his ear, he winced when they all yelled and clapped. "Good, remember this is amateur night and all of these participants are new to this experience. If you would like to be part of this experience we have a sign-up sheet going around." He pointed to a buxom woman in a mask, who held up a clipboard. "If you're the shy type, you can sign-up in the back of the room. We even have private rooms for those that don't like the spotlight, but want to try it. Now, if you will permit me…" He slowly bowed to the crowd.

A beautiful brunette was led onto the stage, blindfolded and naked from the waist up, pasties covering her nipples. She stood in the center of the stage facing the crowd.

"Holy shit," Francesca whispered.

"Hot huh," Dorothy said, watching the scene unfold before her.

A chorus of wows reverberated around the room as another petite woman in spiked boots, a cupless bustier and a leather mask appeared with an arm full of bondage gear.

"Good evening ladies and gentlemen. It's nice to see the house full of such beautiful women." Smiling, she looked again at the tables in the front. "My name is Mistress Rose and this is my pet, Iris. Tonight, she has agreed to receive her discipline in public. Now, I must warn you that she likes it little rough, but since this is your first time, we'll go easy on her."

"Holy shit," another woman at the table whispered. "This is some crazy ass-shit."

"Ten bucks and you can go," Dorothy said putting her hand out.

"No way, I'm good. I'm just sayin' this is some freaky shit."

"Iris, your safe word is…."

"Red, Mistress."

"Ladies and Gentleman, if you hear the word Red, your job is to yell, RED. Okay?" Mistress Kitty said. She smiled and licked her lips.

A low hum washed across the room.

"I'm sorry. I can't hear you." Mistress Kitty cupped her ear and pitched forward dramatically.

"RED."

Goose bumps covered Francesca's arms as she watched the mistress apply clamps to the woman's nipples. Next, the woman's hands were placed in an iron bar contraption, exposing her chest and back more. The mistress tugged on the clamps to check their security and ran her hand over the woman's tight stomach. Slowly, she caressed the woman's ass and then removed her short skirt, exposing a leather thong to the audience.

The crowd watched the mistress skillfully work the flogger over the woman's chest and ass. A bright shade of pink worked its way around her slender body. Francesca watched the intricate pattern of red welts that crisscrossed the naked woman's body and wondered if it hurt. The woman licked her lips and then bit her lower lip. It was clear that Iris was enjoying this torture, and it sent a shiver through Francesca's body. She felt shame when her body tingled in response to seeing the blindfolded woman whipped. Francesca gasped, had she heard her right? Surely, she had been mistaken. Then it happened again.

"Please, ma'am, one more."

Her masked torturer obliged the request, striking at another clear swath on her body.

"I bet you a hundred bucks you couldn't do that." Dorothy whispered in Francesca's ear.

"I bet *you* couldn't do that," Francesca said, pissed that her friend was acting like she could do it.

"I could do that, piece of cake," Dorothy smiled, meeting Francesca's eyes and then ran her tongue over her lips.

Francesca had heard enough. She needed a break and a trip to the ladies room was just what the doctor ordered. Fighting her way past the crowd at the back of the club, she pushed the bathroom door open and sighed. *No line.* The air-conditioned coolness of the bathroom felt refreshing and lucky for her, quieter. Resting against the wall, the chilly tile was a welcome cooling on her back. Her mind was on overload - the flashing lights, the booming bass of the music vibrated through her. The tall, swaggering, darkness of the club owner, Selene, was sexy as hell. She had total bad girl written all over her—so not Francesca's type. Her dark eyes pulled at Francesca. Francesca was naïve when it came to bondage. She'd thought when she entered the club tonight she wanted to keep it that way. Now she wasn't so sure.

The voyeur inside kept her glued to her seat as the scene unfolded before her. Each time the whip landed on its target, it sent a rush through her. She couldn't explain it. Pain wasn't an aphrodisiac to her, but thinking about someone else controlling her had a certain appeal, a certain detachment she might enjoy. Her neat, nice little life was so orderly, it begged for something or someone to come in and turn it upside down. Pulling the stall door shut, she sat down and rested her head in her hands. A few minutes, she only needed a few minutes to recover before rejoining the rowdy table.

The ladies room door opened and a set of distinct footsteps echoed through the room. Peeking through the crack between the door and wall, she recognized Selene washing her hands. Francesca jumped when Selene looked directly at her through the barrier. Thankfully, she turned back to the sink and ignored Francesca. She waited a minute longer and realized she couldn't sit in the stall forever. Eventually a break would send women flooding into the bathroom, so she reluctantly stood, flushed the toilet and came face-to-face with *walking sex*.

"Hi, Francesca, right?"

"Hi," Francesca said, a bit embarrassed, caught

in the bathroom just sitting.

Selene dabbed at a red spot on her blouse and then looked at Francesca again.

"You okay?"

"Oh, yeah, I just needed a break from the group and since I don't smoke." She slapped her chest. "Asthma. I didn't want to hangout in the smoking area. It's nice in here though."

Now she felt silly. It was a restroom, not a lounge found in some ritzy club or hotel.

Selene turned around and gave the room a once over. "Well, I guess I don't need to do that remodel I was considering." She laughed and resumed dabbing at the stain.

"Here, let me help you. Is that club soda" Francesca pointed to the bottle on the counter.

"Yeah, Jax said it would get this wine stain out."

"Kinda messy are ya?"

"Actually, your friend did this."

"Oh, sorry. She can be a little wild when she's had too much to drink."

"A little?"

"Okay, a lot." Francesca knew there would be a story behind this stain. There always was when it came to Dorothy. Without thinking, Francesca reached her hand under Selene's blouse cupping the stain.

"Hand me that bottle." she said nodding at it.

"I can do this," Selene seemed uncomfortable.

Francesca's finger brushed against the pale skin that was in direction contrast with Selene's dark eyes, and straight, shiny hair, so black the tinted highlights glinted blue in the light. She fumbled with the club soda, and the spill soaked through Selene's blouse, revealing the outline of a dark nipple through the now sheer material that lay on Selene's bare breast.

Selene sucked in a deep breath. "Oh that's cold."

"Oh sorry, sorry." Francesca grabbed a paper towel and dabbed at the wet spot over the erect nipple.

Selene stopped her. "Here, I'll get that."

"Of course, sorry."

"It's not your fault."

"Are you okay?"

A hand on her arm pulled Francesca from her daydream and back to the present.

"I'm sorry?" Francesca blushed at the touch from the club owner.

"I said, are you okay?" Selene removed her hand. "Would you like me to call one of your friends over? Do you need to sit down?"

"Huh? No, no I'm fine. I was just lost in thought I guess. I'm sorry for what happened back at the table. Dorothy has boundary issues, and the other ladies… well I guess doing research for a living doesn't make for great social skills."

"I noticed, but you seem to be able to handle yourself." Selene smiled.

A jolt speared right through Francesca in response; a twinge of guilt she was sure.

"Oh, well…I'm…I mean…I get out…uh, I don't get out…out, but I do seem to be able to keep myself from looking like an ass, luckily." She looked down at her shoes. Now she was a blubbering idiot, but at least she wasn't still staring at the club owner's chest anymore. It wasn't her fault, they were eye level… besides…oh it didn't matter. She was way out of Francesca's league. Tall, dark and gorgeous never went for pale, short and shapely.

"Well, I have to get back to work. It was nice to

meet you…" Selene offered her hand.

"Oh right, sorry. Francesca. Remember, I told you out there?" Now she was sure the woman was out of her league, not a second thought.

"I thought you said people called you Francesca?"

"They do, I mean some people do, mostly the people I work with do, but…" *shut up.* "Francesca's fine."

With that, she turned on her heel and dashed from the restroom leaving Selene behind shaking her head.

Chapter Eight

The folded parchment sat dead center of her desk. The red wax seal, denoted it was from someone in the coven or at least someone affiliated with the coven. Selene sat down in her leather chair, steepled her fingers and ran her lips back and forth over the tips.

Studying the paper, she knew that whoever wrote the letter was making a request. She wondered if the person writing knew the price they would have to pay for her services? More often than not, money wasn't the issue. The issue was usually the *who*.

Picking up the letter she studied the seal. Typical shield with a hand thrusting a sword upwards, denoted a Scottish clan. She hadn't heard from the Scots in decades. There were few in their ranks, but those few in the coven considered themselves a long line of warriors and handled their own *family* business.

Breaking the wax seal in half, the rush of cologne and sweat pulled at her nostrils as she unfolded the parchment. *Damn men*, she thought, *can't they do anything in moderation?*

Selene,

It's a sad day when I am in need of your services. Unfortunately, I am desperate. I await your terms and conditions for employment.

Respectfully,

Ian.

Selene tapped the envelope against the desk. What could Ian want from her? He'd been silent for so long she thought him dead and gone. Though an announcement usually followed the death of her kind, even if it weaved its way through the grapevine. But, money was money and what did she care who employed her as long as they paid?

She picked up her phone and dialed the number on the letterhead.

"Hello." The soft voice on the other end sounded young.

"May I speak to Ian, please?"

"A moment, please."

Selene thought she could hear blankets rustling in the background and a muffed squeal. Ian was a dog to the n'th degree, so it wasn't a surprise if he was bedding a new conquest.

"Ian, here." Wisps of his Irish brogue still laced his words. It took work to keep an accent alive this long and Selene wondered if he kept it for the ladies.

"Ian, Selene."

Silence and more blankets rustling before Ian said anything else. "Selene. You got my request."

"I got a note requesting my services. What can I do for you, Ian?"

"I'd like to meet in person, Selene. This is a delicate matter."

Selene didn't usually meet with her clients. The nature of her business made her a target for those that might want to kill *her*.

"I don't meet with my clients, Ian. You know that. Besides, I'm assuming you remember the routine. Half up front, the rest upon completion."

Selene kept the detail vague when she spoke on the phone. She never knew who might be listening and she didn't need more problems than she already had. She'd refused more jobs than she'd taken lately. Death was a dirty business—literally and figuratively. Moving away from it and into more lucrative enterprises helped line her pockets now. Besides, she liked the way she slept at night. The constant need to look over her shoulder kept her from becoming involved with anyone, fearful they would become a target just because they'd been seen with her.

"I know, but I thought you might make an exception this once."

"No."

More silence. She was starting to get a feeling it might be best to let this job go to someone else. Her gut was often right, but she would let Ian confirm that for her.

"Okay, I understand. Look, I've got a problem that needs a resolution. The coven won't handle the interloper so I need to handle it."

More silence.

"You still there?" He sounded like he was cupping the phone for privacy.

"Yep."

"Selene, I'm in a bad way here. I need someone to disappear as soon as possible. The bastard's giving me fits and Van der Plume won't budge an inch."

"Details, Ian."

"I've got this *chancer*, De Marcus..." Selene's

ears perked up. "trying to put the pinch on me. Says I owe him."

Selene knew she would take this job. Her gut said no, but she wanted De Marcus' head on a platter. Especially if it meant getting AJ off her back. Selene figured that the word was out that she was after De Marcus. What she didn't know was how deep the word went. Hell, you'd have to be living under a rock not to know she was after the bastard.

"I need to ask you some questions before I decide whether or not to take the job."

"Aw, come on, Selene. I'm feelin' the screw here. I need someone to handle to this tool, before he tries anything else."

"Look, answer my questions truthfully and this will go faster. Bulldog me and I'll hang up."

"Right, right. Let me put some clothes on."

"Why, I can't see you?"

"Well aren't you a lucky girl? You just might swoon if you saw my—"

"Stop. I'm not interested in your manhood or lack of it."

"Aw stop, Selene. You know I'm bigger than an ox."

"Could we get to the questions, if you don't mind, of course. This *is* my dime."

"Oh, right. Well, get on with it girl. I'm as decent as I'm going to get in this lifetime."

Selene wanted to punch the arrogant bastard, but that would have to wait until they were face to face. "Where are you?"

"In me *gaff*."

"No shit, you *gowl*." Selene knew enough Irish to be offensive, which always seemed to be foreplay for some guys. Ian could have easily said he was at home, but slipping back into his Irish meant he'd been drinking.

"Aww, you're a *feek* after me own heart. Careful, Selene, I'll win you over yet."

"Doubtful, Ian, now let's get on with it. Where are you?"

"I'm in the Low valley."

Low valley was vampire slang for a place at a higher altitude where it was damn near impossible for an average human to find. The lighter atmosphere made breathing difficult and a house situated between mountain peaks often led to darker days no matter the time of year.

"What low valley, Ian?"

"I'm over in Donner."

The irony wasn't lost on Selene. Donner was in the Sierra foothills on the way to Tahoe, named after the people who reportedly saved themselves by eating their fellow travelers. *Disgusting.*

"Seriously?"

"What?"

"Are you trying to be a smart-ass?"

"You'd be amazed how many people, especially ours, who avoid the place like the plague. They think it's running with ghosts and beasties. So it keeps me safe and the girls love that they can scream their heads off when I fuck 'em. Besides, it's cold and high enough that I don't have neighbors."

"But it's so damn cold."

"Yeah, isn't it great."

Selene preferred the warmth of the coast, the fog giving just enough protection to those who didn't want all that sunshine. She'd lived all over the world and avoided destinations that took her anywhere close to the equator. Central American was out, so was the African continent. *Besides*, she thought, *all that sand was just too...* It didn't matter, she'd made her choice, and unless something came up to change that, she was content where she was, for now.

"Selene?"

"Yeah, I'm here."

"So, I guess I'll come to you then."

"The Dungeon. It'll take you what, four maybe five hours?"

"If I fly." Ian's implication was clear. "I've got a damn appointment I can't get out of Selene. Besides, can you give me a couple of days to get the funds? I don't have green on me."

"How many days, Ian?"

"I need to go down into the city for my appointment and then I need to get the check. So a couple is all I'll need?"

"Do whatever. If you're not here by..." Selene pulled her sleeve back and continued, "six on Thursday, don't bother."

"I'll be there."

"Since you're going to the bank bring cash, no checks, or international drafts." Selene didn't need the money, but if someone paid, they rarely backed out and she hated when someone got cold feet.

"The usual?"

"It's gonna cost you more since it's De Marcus."

"But—"

"No, but. If you want this bastard dead, you need to pay. I have a full dance card and you're asking me to add you."

"Fine, what'll it be?"

Negotiating was one of Selene's pet peeves. She waited for Ian to quote a price and then with a fudge factor of five they finally agreed to an amount Selene knew was absurdly gross. Ian could afford it. The fact that he didn't flinch when she countered made her wish she had bounced higher.

Hanging up she suddenly needed a stiff drink and a diversion. One she could easily get, the other would have to wait until a more opportune time presented her with a willing participant.

Chapter Nine

Francesca sat on her sofa with her feet tucked underneath her. Her mind and body felt like it had run a marathon tonight. Between the loud music, the alcohol and the exchanges that had played out on stage she *still* couldn't wrap her mind around what she'd seen earlier. The logical part of her brain could rationalize the need for some people to experience pain. She guessed it was a need to release control, but to surrender total control to someone else involved a massive amount of trust and Francesca just wasn't that trusting. Then to top it all off there was the bombshell club owner, Selene. *Sex on a stick.* Wow, what she would give to see some of that a little more up close and personal. She had to wonder if Selene was into the kinky stuff, she did own the club, right? Therefore, that must mean she was some type of deviant, too. What else could it mean?

"Hey, how was the club?" Francesca's roommate, Daphne asked. They'd lived together since college. Daphne was a product of the "me" generation, given everything by her parents, and that allowed her to spend her time on whatever social cause she fancied. Save the Oceans, Green Peace, anything that screamed *activist* was Daphne's agenda. Francesca always wondered why someone like Daphne hung out with a nerd like her. Daphne's smoldering, sexy good looks got her into places Francesca could only imagine. But they'd gotten along so well they decided to continue that tradition when they graduated.

"Oh, it was…interesting."

"Really? Spill," she said, sitting on the sofa and pulling her feet tighter under her.

"It was fine, really."

"Oh come on, stop being coy and tell me every little detail. I've always wanted to go to a place like that but Mark isn't into that kinda stuff." Daphne wiggled her manicured eyebrows.

Francesca wasn't trying to be coy, she just wasn't sure how to described something so full of debauchery that it defied explanation.

"Oh there had to be one interesting thing tonight." Daphne leaned in resting on the arm of the sofa. "There wasn't even *one* cool thing about tonight, not one?"

"Well…if you're into that sorta thing I guess it was interesting."

"Okay, so what does *geeky* girl think about the night?"

They invented a game in college where if Francesca found it embarrassing and couldn't talk about something, she would respond as "geeky girl", her other persona. It sounded silly, but by making a game out of it, she found it easier to discuss difficult topics like sex, the opposite sex and her lack of dates. Her nerdy tendencies kept her focused, on time and able to earn a decent salary, but not quite enough to live on her own, at least that's what she told herself. Besides, she liked the comfort and security of having someone else in the house. She'd been left alone as a child and she wasn't ready for more solitude, not yet. It also limited her social skills, her ability to date, working out or being the social butterfly like Daphne.

"I'm glad I went. I've never seen anything like it before, but I doubt I'll ever go again."

"Really, so want happened?" Daphne plopped down next to her, grabbed a pillow and hugged it close.

"It was unbelievable. They had this woman named Mistress Rose and she came out and whipped this guy. He asked for it..."

"What? No way."

"Yep, she had this long whip that she flicked out over the audience. We could feel the wind snap above us as she flicked it back, cracking it above our heads."

"No shit?"

"Yep." Francesca nodded. "Then she used it to whip this guy who was tied up on an X-shaped thingie. He would beg her to hit him. I couldn't believe it."

"No shit."

"No shit."

"What else happened?"

"Oh, then Dorothy harassed the owner, as she always does. It was embarrassing, *as usual*."

"What? I thought she was married?"

"She is and you want to hear the topper?"

"Sure."

"It was a woman."

"Who was a woman?"

"The owner."

"The owner of the bondage club is a woman? Wow, who would have guessed a woman would own a bondage club?"

"I know, right?"

Francesca hoped that Daphne wouldn't ask any more questions. She had to admit the club and the actions contained inside its dark, secret-filled walls had an attraction she couldn't explain. She hadn't grown up in a repressed house, quite the opposite. With three brothers she often found herself the butt of their vulgarity laced humor. She would come home and find jock straps hanging from her bedroom door handle, her brothers daring her to touch the filthy things. Playboys randomly tucked in her clothes drawers. Looking back now it was her first hint that she liked girls. Maybe not the spread-eagle types displayed voyeuristically in the pages, but the kind that walked her high school campus. Her secret crush – a cheerleader that was nice to everyone, had a bubbly personality and a kind word for the *geek* with braces. Innocently enough, she had set the standard by which Francesca would judge all women by from then on. However, her attraction to the club owner defied explanation. The dark undertones of the woman made Francesca tingle. It was like looking over the edge of a cliff and knowing if you stayed rooted to where stood you were okay, but lean out a bit too far and you risked falling. Selene was edgy, intense and sexy as hell. The complete opposite of Anita, the high school cheerleader. Francesca didn't have to worry, there was no way someone like Selene fell for girls like her. It just didn't happen and playing with fire wasn't her style. A girl could dream, though, and Francesca was sure Selene would fuel her fantasies for weeks to come.

"Hey, the lights are on but no one's home." Daphne's snapping fingers brought Francesca back into the conversation and focused back where Daphne always wanted it.

"Sorry, I was just thinking..." Francesca thought about how she would finish the sentence without giving up too much information.

"About the club owner, huh?"

"What? No."

"So, what does she look like?"

"Who?" Francesca said, before taking a sip of her diet soda.

"Oh, that good huh?"

"No, I mean yes, but—"

"Spill little sister." Daphne settled in, pushing her feet under Francesca. Clearly, she wasn't going to be deterred so there was no use trying to be vague. Francesca knew she would hound her until she whittled every little detail possible out of her. She felt like lying, but she wasn't good at it and Daphne knew it.

"Not much to tell really. She's okay looking, I guess. Average, tall—"

"Fat, skinny, long hair short hair, what did she wear?"

"Seriously?"

"Aren't you the least bit intrigued about why a woman would own a bondage club? I mean think about it, it's a dude kind of thing. Don't you think?"

Francesca hadn't dissected it that far. In fact, she hadn't had time to really give it that kind of in-depth thought. She was good at analyzing a situation, searching for the obvious and expecting the unexpected. It's what made her good at her job, but she had to admit, a woman owning a bondage club was kind of edgy, raw and completely unpredicted. Maybe that's why she was so embarrassed by her co-worker's behavior. If Selene had been a man and Dorothy had treated him like that she wouldn't have had a problem with it—at least she didn't think she would. Was she being sexist?

"Yeah, I guess. I didn't really think about it like that, Daphne."

"Oh, I want to go. You have to take me."

"I don't know…" Francesca felt herself shying away from a repeat of the night's activities, sort of. Goose bumps prickled her skin. *Ah, a visceral reaction is never a good sign*, she thought, rubbing her arms. Selene's touch had been like a spark charging through her body. Her nipples tightened instantly and she body flushed from her toes to the hair's standing on her head. Francesca had to admit there was an entrancing quality about Selene. She still felt the rush of touching her in the bathroom.

"Cold, sweetie?"

"Yeah, a little," Francesca lied.

Daphne wrapped her tight in a hug and rocked her. "It'll be fun, I won't embarrass you like Dorothy did."

Hmmm. That's what you think. It never works out that way when sexy, debauchery is involved.

When Daph set her mind on something, she rarely let it rest. So how was she going to get out of this? The thought of seeing Selene again had its merits, even if she watched from a distance. Selene would never have to know she was even there. Enough of the club was kept in deliberate darkness that she was sure she could hide. What was she thinking? This was creepy, provocative, and not something she would do, but the more she thought about the club and it's dark, sultry owner, the more she wanted to see her again. Not talk, just see.

Chapter Ten

So, what were the results of the new blood tests?" AJ leafed through the folder. She pulled out a spreadsheet and ran her finger down the page.

"Well, Ms. Lockwood, the results are promising. It's the strongest concentration yet. A small amount can be reconstituted to almost ten times. The transfusion process has no effect on the blood. It's really fantastic and will save lives in the field."

"Interesting…the purity?" AJ studied the next sheet and then tossed the folder on her desk. Picking up the tin of red capsules, she moved them around and paused to focus on her lead researcher, Dr. Francesca Swartz. "Have we tested them in a real environment?"

AJ had been pressing her researchers to develop a stronger, purer blood concentrate. They had been working on something stronger to sustain her longer, to avoid feeding on warm human blood, or at least warm blood. The product she bought for research was passable, but it hindered her ability to be more mobile. She'd conditioned herself to stop feeding, but in a crisis, she found the cravings difficult to ignore, and lately the De Marcus situation had put her in crisis mode.

"The purity is almost ninety percent when reconstituted. As for testing, we've completed baseline testing and we're ready to move forward with the military research center. They've expressed an interest in taking it into the field." Francesca read through her notes. "Since this is a purer version of what they're already using, we're pretty confident that they'll just replace the current supply with this."

AJ liked Dr. Swartz. She was a research genius and AJ swooped her up as soon as she graduated from Harvard Medical School. AJ had been aware of the blood experiments Dr. Swartz did at the Thorndike Laboratory at Harvard. It had taken some convincing to get Francesca to reconsider the offer made by the Blood Center of Wisconsin, but money was no object for AJ and she wouldn't take no for an answer. The deciding factor had been a state of the art lab with the latest equipment and no budget. All things that kept most labs mired in fundraising and partnering with big businesses to get the much-needed money for research.

"This is great news, Dr. Swartz. What's the production schedule looking like?" AJ counted ten capsules in her hand. With the new formula these might last her twenty days. If she rationed them, they could last longer.

"These take longer to process. The potency makes it critical that we don't skip any critical steps."

"How long?"

"If we have a steady supply of blood, we can probably produce…one hundred capsules per batch."

The intercom buzzed. "Ms. Lockwood, You have a visitor."

"I don't have an appointment *now* do I?"

"No, you don't have anything else on your calendar for today."

"Then tell them to schedule an appointment," AJ

said, turning the intercom off. The intercom buzzed again. "Yes."

"I'm sorry Ms. Lockwood, *she* said you need to see her now."

Selene pushed past Maggie and into her office. She started to speak then appeared to stop when she spotted Francesca.

AJ watched with curiosity as Francesca flushed and then cast her eyes down, avoiding Selene's gaze.

"Selene, I'm right in the middle of a meeting, couldn't this have waited?"

No, I'm afraid it couldn't.

AJ wondered why Selene wasn't talking, but poking around in her mind explained volumes.

Get out of my head, AJ

"Dr. Swartz, may I introduce Selene Hightower. She's one of my oldest friends." AJ turned towards Selene and motioned towards her researcher. "Selene, this is Dr. Francesca Swartz."

"Dr. Swartz." Selene extended her hand, but refused to make eye contact with the doctor. *This is highly embarrassing.* "It's a pleasure to meet you."

AJ wasn't sure what was going on, but Francesca's hesitancy to shake Selene's hand and her sudden silence was interesting. Tension rolled off Selene in waves, which wasn't something new, but she was more anxious than usual. Oh, something was definitely going on here and AJ was going to find out what that was.

"Ms. Hightower, it's a pleasure to meet you. If that will be all, Ms. Locke, I need to get back to the lab."

She was out the door and gone before AJ could say anything.

"What the hell was that all about Selene?"

"What?"

"I heard what you were thinking. Do you know the good doctor?"

"Not really."

"That's not what you were thinking just now."

Selene became a little more aggressive and advanced on her. "Let it go AJ"

"Calm down, big girl." AJ sat on the couch trying to look as non-threatening as possible. "Since you've canceled my meeting with Dr. Swartz and you refuse to tell me why her body went off the charts when you came in, why don't you tell me why you're here?"

Selene paced the office like a cage animal. AJ could barely make sense of her racing thoughts. Something about a guy named Ian, De Marcus and then a flood of emotions about Francesca. *De Marcus!*

"What's going on with De Marcus, Selene?"

"Stay out of my head AJ. Fuck." Selene took a deep breath and slowed her pacing.

"Okay, so…"

"I got a call from this guy, Ian. Seems someone's tapping him and he wants this guy dead. The guy, De Marcus."

"Okay, so…"

"So, I think it's a ruse." Selene pulled a chair around and sat facing AJ

"Color me stupid, but why do you think it's a trap?" AJ wanted De Marcus and she was willing to do whatever it took to kill the bastard. Trap or no trap.

"Just a feeling." Selene pulled her fingers through her long dark locks and then flicked the ends back.

"I'm going to need more than that, Selene."

"The word is out that we want De Marcus. How

easy would it be to have someone set me up on the pretense of hiring me and then off me? I haven't heard from Ian in decades and then out of the clear blue he sends me a note that he wants to hire me for a job. Then he names De Marcus as his problem."

"Yeah, but why would he tell you the problem is De Marcus?"

"Exactly."

"Because he wants you to take the job, that's why." AJ said, stating what she saw was the obvious answer. "He has to know that you want De Marcus. Would you have taken the job if it was someone else?"

"Probably not. I told him the last time I did work for him not to call me, ever."

"Hmm, so he tells you it's De Marcus 'cause he knows you wouldn't do the job otherwise. I'd say he's pretty smart. He knows you won't work for him and he knows he needs someone good, very good and you're the only one who can get 'em."

"Maybe."

"Who better to hire than someone who has an axe to grind? Revenge is always a great incentive. If you won't take the job I'll do it. I want De Marcus dead, period."

"You paid me to kill him and I'm going to kill him, so stop with the bullshit. Besides, you have Clarissa to worry about."

"When do you meet with Ian?" AJ knew that she wanted to be there when Selene met with Ian. Selene was right, it could be a set up. They couldn't be too careful.

"Thursday, six p.m.."

"I should be back from the coven by then and maybe you won't have to meet with Ian."

"What? Wait, you're not going to the coven. I don't trust Van der Plume."

"I'm going and you aren't going to stop me. I want to look at that little worm's face and confront him. He needs to know who he's fucking with." AJ's voice filled with hatred. "I'm tired of the coven's bullshit. They're antiquated fucks that need to die. They're the whole reason De Marcus is alive and we're watching over our shoulder every second of the day. Clarissa deserves a life without wondering if De Marcus is going to pop in when he feels like it and fuck with us. I want answers."

"I don't like this, AJ."

"I didn't ask you if you liked this. I just told you I want answers. I don't need your blessing to go to the coven, Selene."

"No, you're a big girl all right. Big enough to fuck shit up and get your ass in a sling."

"I'm not asking you to bail me out. I don't plan on pissing anyone off, I just want De Marcus and some answers."

"Does Clarissa know you're going to the coven?"

"No, and she isn't going to find out, is she?" AJ walked to her desk and sat down. "I'm leaving in the morning and I'll be back in time for dinner. She'll never even know I was gone."

Chapter Eleven

Clarissa had been running errands all day before her night class. Dry cleaning, getting her car washed and shopping almost made her feel like a normal human being. Almost. She hadn't spoken to AJ all day and wouldn't see her until late tonight after class. Their jobs had been one compromise they had made to each other. *Keep some facsimile of normalcy, even if someone was out to kill you, who else has to live like that?* Clarissa wondered. Clarissa parked her car in her usual spot, right under the lamppost, the light illuminating her car. Safety. AJ drilled it into her head constantly. She arrived early enough to park close to her office and classrooms. The parking garage was not an option. She hated the enclosed space and when she had used the garage before it had resulted in flashback to her former life with De Marcus. So, no garage, no flashbacks. Checking her phone one last time before turning it to silent, she noticed a message from AJ.

Ms. Du Monte, your presence is requested for a lovely dinner, fireside at 6 p.m. Please be prompt as the owner hates to wait to see you.

Love isn't a word spoken between two people, it's the realization that you couldn't survive without them. See you at six.

AJ

Clarissa smiled at the text and sent a quick response back.

Dinner with the most enchanting woman I know sounds wonderful. See you at six.
Love
C

AJ had a way with flowery language. She always had, even when they first met.

A long determined hand reached out as Clarissa sat down. "Pardon me. I don't believe we have met yet? My name is Alexandra Locke, and you are?" The last word hung on a perfect French accent.

Clarissa stood quickly as though she were meeting the King of France. "My apologies, Madam Locke, my name is Clarissa Dumonte. It's my pleasure of course to meet you."

"I don't know why it would be your pleasure, my dear, but it is kind of you to say." Chuckling, Alexandra guided Clarissa back into her seat. "Please sit down. People might think that I am someone special and wonder why you stood so quickly. Please," Alexandra said, as Clarissa watched her glance around the room, obviously uncomfortable with Clarissa's response.

"So, Mademoiselle Dumonte, please tell me you are not Monsieur De Marcus's new engagement?"

"Engagement?" Clarissa looked over at the arrogant man Alexandra referred to.

"Yes, engagement. Monsieur De Marcus has quite the reputation as a ladies' man and you seem rather, well, let us just say you don't seem to be his usual type." Alexandra looked directly at Clarissa, making her blush.

"I am sure I don't know what you mean, Madame Locke but —"

"Please, call me Alexandra. The other is so formal. Besides, be honest. Monsieur De Marcus is so…well, he is a cad and you don't seem to be in need of a cad. Am I right?"

AJ had enchanted Clarissa from the start. Her demeanor, her eloquence, and that French accent pulled at Clarissa the moment they met. How far would she fall? She found out later that night when she was alone with AJ on the balcony.

Clarissa leaned back against the bulk of the ornate balustrade and reached behind with her hands, balancing herself. She let her head slowly roll back and took a deep breath. The perfumed scent of wisteria in full bloom hung in the air. It felt good to relax and enjoy the quiet of the evening, even if it was for a short time. Soon, she would be home in bed, wishing she had never accepted her father's suggestion of a date with Monsieur De Marcus.

"You know, you should be careful out here unprotected, Mademoiselle."

Clarissa could barely make out the silhouette of a person standing in the shadows.

"I'm sorry. I didn't know anyone was out here. I didn't mean to intrude on your privacy."

"Please, don't apologize. I was only enjoying the evening, as you were." Alexandra moved out of the shadows slowly and stopped next to Clarissa. She was close enough to recognize the perfume, hints of honeysuckle.

"Besides I am sure you must struggle to endure the insufferable condition of your sentence, seated between those remarkable specimens of the male

species. You are in need of the quiet more than I." She turned to go back inside.

"Please, wait. Don't go...I mean, you don't have to go in just because I am here. The porch is big enough for two, or more."

Clarissa was thankful for the darkness. The blush that seemed to accompany a conversation with Alexandra crept up Clarissa's neck again. She could feel Alexandra's eyes on her. The thought made her shiver. Clarissa told herself it was the thought of talking to an unaccompanied woman that made her curious. It was rare in Parisian society that women went to parties unescorted. It was thought to be in bad taste. The idea that a woman was unable to secure a man to escort her meant something was wrong. She should stay home to be thought of as respectable. The fact that Madame Locke did not stay home intrigued Clarissa. At least that's what she told herself. No, there was something more about Madame Locke, but Clarissa couldn't quite put her finger on it. The silence between the two was almost deafening as Clarissa was startled back to reality by an owl flying by.

"Ah, we seem to have company."

Clarissa looked around and didn't see anyone.

"Excuse me, but I don't see anyone."

"The owl. Don't you hear him?" Leaning in, she whispered into Clarissa's ear, "There, don't you hear him?" Alexandra's nearness was overwhelming Clarissa and she took a step back, only to be stopped by the balustrade behind her.

"Relax, you aren't for dinner tonight...." Alexandra continued, "...the mouse, he is dinner."

Clarissa felt a wave of calm wash over her as she inhaled Alexandra's perfume. Relaxing against *the bulk of the balcony, she turned to see Alexandra staring at her again. She returned the gaze, determined not to weaken under the intense scrutiny. Her gaze roamed over Alexandra's face. A smile meandered across Alexandra's lips. Her teeth oddly reflecting the moon's light. A tingle ran down her spine as Alexandra ran her tongue along her top lip.*

Her mind often relived those early memories, the purest love one could have for another individual, before De Marcus ruined it. Clarissa had resigned herself to the fact that AJ would outlive her once AJ revealed her secret. She just didn't know the plague would end her young existence so early, that was until De Marcus turned her. She now knew he had done it out of spite and murdered her family, blaming it on a vengeful AJ. He told her that if AJ couldn't have Clarissa, then AJ would have her family. The heartbreak had been almost insurmountable, but she had resigned herself to her fate and De Marcus' pervert and evil twists.

That was all behind her now and she could move on with her life with AJ. She would sleep easier when De Marcus was caught, but she felt completely safe with AJ and the men she hired to keep her that way. Suddenly, her skin tingled. Standing up straight she looked around and saw one of AJ's hired guns. They locked eyes and he nodded at her. *Hmmm, must be him,* she thought bending over to grab her backpack and briefcase. Keeping with their own kind kept questions to a minimum if something out of the ordinary happened. The threat of death from an elder was a powerful incentive to keep their charge well taken care of—the money didn't hurt either.

She said hello to nearly every student in her

major during the short walk to the office. When she finally reached her office she tossed her stuff on her couch and plopped down in her chair. The day had barely started and she was already tired. The end of the semester would be a godsend. Her skin prickled again. Something wasn't right.

A knock on her open door made her jump. "Hello, sorry I didn't mean to scare you. I just wanted to come by and introduce myself. I'm taking Carol's classes over for the rest of the semester. My name's Marshall."

The young man stuck his hand out and smiled at Clarissa.

❧ ❧ ❧ ❧

AJ grabbed her carry-on and set it by the door. She hadn't told Clarissa where she was going when Clarissa left for school today. She'd thought better of it. She didn't want her to worry and Selene could be wrong about Butch. She was sure when she met with him he would see reason. De Marcus was a blight on the coven and a cancer needed to be removed before it grew out of control. All she wanted to do was protect what was hers, Clarissa.

She'd be gone and back before Clarissa got home and none the wiser. The intercom buzzed, alerting her that her ride had arrived. Her private jet stood ready and another car waited at the other end. Up, down and back again. Easy enough. At least she hoped it would be that easy.

AJ filled the two-hour flight with paperwork that had gone begging for far too long. Her assistant had been on her to replace Kevin - her right hand man, but AJ just couldn't do it. His treachery devastated her. He had been with her almost two decades. He had buried himself so deep into her world that she had no idea he was the mole working for De Marcus. Finding him dead at his own hand had taken what little joy AJ would have gotten out of killing the rat.

"Ms. Locke, we're arriving so if you'll buckle up and stow your things we'll be landing shortly."

"Thank you."

AJ could feel herself amping up for the impending meeting with Gaylord, or Butch, as he supposedly wanted to be addressed. *Pompous ass.* If things went well she would leave knowing where De Marcus was and with the blessing of the coven to eliminate the pain in the ass.

The plane finally coasted to a stop. She pulled on her leather jacket, her stiletto firmly tucked in the inner pocket, grabbed her briefcase and cell phone, and disembarked. A four-wheel drive waited for her at the bottom of the staircase. Tucked away in the most remote location she'd ever seen sat *nothing*, if you didn't know what you were looking for. Buried deep into the mountain, the coven had carved out a very nice existence for their members. Stately, ornate and opulent, were all words that would barely describe the interior, because there was no exterior except a mountain. The old military bunker had been picked up when the government dumped excess property. No one the wiser, Butch had put the bid in under a dummy corporation and bam, the coven had a new pristine home far from the reach of the very government that wanted them dead. It was dark, remote and amazing. She wished she'd thought of it. Maybe at some point she would pick one up.

The world was spinning off its axis. The financial crisis was hitting both home and abroad, the job market and the next looming communicable disease was just around the corner. She suspected it wouldn't be long before the government took control of the world's resources. They were already reading emails, cell phone conversations, accessing bank records and even home computers. They had their hands on too much personal information, so putting together a war on vampires would be easy. Thanks to the way the coven was running its business, they were giving the government plenty of reasons to put out a war on vampires. They'd assimilated into higher levels of government: local, federal and the military, but it would be a civil war of epic proportions. The coven knew that and assumed the odds were weighted heavily in their favor, the endless life and all. Without humans, and her research, they'd eventually starve to death. It might take half a century, but it would happen. As for making a move on her research, the coven knew little about what she did. She had complete autonomy. She'd had a benevolent master who'd set her free when he'd died. She was one of the lucky ones. Now she wanted to give Clarissa that same opportunity. Killing De Marcus would do that.

Pulling a tab from her pocket, she snapped it and placed it under her tongue. Feeding time. Energy surged through her instantly. The new blood formula was working better than she had anticipated. A process of dehydration, and then rehydration through the body's system made the blood the ultimate food. Fewer feedings, longer lasting energy and more time in between capsules all made for a vampire super food. In the wrong hands...that wasn't an option.

Any other time AJ would love the drive. The lush green scenery was breathtaking, the brisk mountain air, a brush of snow on the trees. It all made for a Christmas card style landscape. In fact she wished Clarissa was sitting right next to her, but she had some unfinished business with the coven and then maybe they could finally take that vacation they'd been planning.

A man wearing camouflage fatigues standing in front of a barricade flagged her down and she slowed to a stop. Not a vampire. There were few light walkers and that was AJ's advantage.

"Can I help you miss?" His face was covered so making an identification later would prove difficult.

Yes, of course you can, AJ crept into the man's mind. *You'll let me pass and forget I was here.*

"Let me move the barricade. Down about a quarter mile you'll see a fallen tree, turn left and continue for about a half mile. You'll see a boulder off to the left, look for a quick right. If you're not careful you'll miss it."

Thank you. AJ closed the bond. She smiled and was ready to leave when he said one last thing.

"There are only five ways into the coven, but a hidden passage lies directly below the master's chambers. He often takes women through there when he's done with them."

AJ furrowed her eyebrows at the useless information. Oftentimes someone she melded with gave more information than she needed. She called it diarrhea of the brain, a brain dump, basically. The human condition had a guilty need to purge itself when she bonded with them, it seemed.

"Thank you, I'll be on my way. Have a good day,

officer."

"Yes, ma'am, you too." He returned to his position and didn't move.

Creepy. If this kept up, she was sure she wasn't coming back.

※ ※ ※ ※

Clarissa stared at the offered hand. What did he mean he was taking Carol's classes for the rest of the semester? Where was Carol? She'd never leave without telling Clarissa. Something wasn't making sense.

"What's happened to Carol?"

"Don't know. The dean called me and asked if I was available, and boom, I was," he said almost proud of himself. "I think he said something about her father taking ill." Shrugging his shoulders, he stared at Clarissa and then flashed a toothy grin. "So, guess it's you and me in the Lit department till summer."

"Yeah, I guess it is." Clarissa suddenly got a sickening feeling. Carol's father had died years ago and her mother was her only living relative. Someone was lying, Carol, the dean or this guy, but she wouldn't find out until she went to the dean's office in the morning. Besides, this guy was too perfect, to nice, to pale. The only way to find out was to… Pulling her hand from her pocket she grabbed his and the jolt was instantaneous. She absorbed his energy and shook his hand firmly. He was a vamp, a young one, so she doubted he had picked up on her essence, but he was around for a reason. It was just too coincidental that he showed up to take over Carol's classes.

"Clarissa Du Monte," she said, removing her hand from his sweaty grip.

He cocked his head, then looked at the door and shot her a quizzical look. Pointing to the door, he said, "But the door says, De Marcus."

"I recently got married." Clarissa lied. Who was he to questions what she said? She was sure the firm tone made it clear it wasn't up for discussion. "Well, if you'll excuse me I need to prepare for class. I'm sure you have to get ready as well." Shuffling some papers on her desk she was sure she had dismissed the interloper, but he plopped down on her sofa.

"Nope, I did all that last night. I'm ready. My mom said I was born ready. Said I came out ready to greet the world and take it on."

"How nice, but—"

"Hey how would you like to get some coffee after class, Professor Du Monte? I know this great little coffee shop close to campus. I see the students there all the time, so you know it must be good if they're fillin' up the place."

She turned her attention to the talking head, wanting to be rude, but it just wasn't her style. Besides, what was that old saying–keep your friends close and your enemies closer? Well, until she knew better this guy was the enemy. That still didn't mean she had to have coffee with him.

"I'm sorry, I have dinner plans with my wife."

Marshall sat stunned for a moment, after closing his gaping mouth, he gracefully recovered enough to at least blush.

"Oh, I'm sorry. I didn't know. I mean, I hope you didn't think I was trying to pick-up on you or anything when I asked you out for coffee. I was just trying to be collegial, that's all. Hey, it's cool." Standing, he pulled at the legs of his pants and practically ran to the door.

"You know I just realized I do have a little bit of prep for the class. Hey, it was nice to meet you. Let's get that coffee soon though, okay?"

The only thing missing was the two finger salute men like that shot at women when they suddenly found out they didn't stand a chance with them. Weird…no it was beyond weird. There was no doubt in Clarissa's mind it was all an act. From the impish grin to the "let me show you how suave I am" lines he was throwing around. She pulled her cell phone from her purse and dialed AJ's number but it instantly went to voice mail. Odd. She tried again and it happened again. Dialing AJ's office, she got Maggie. Now she was perplexed.

"Maggie? Why isn't AJ answering her phone?"

"I don't know, she called and said she had an appointment out all day and would be in the office tomorrow. I thought maybe she was playing hookie with you."

Clarissa could hear the smile in Maggie's voice. She loved Maggie. It was clear she kept all AJ's secrets and loved her anyway. Unlike Kevin who had practically destroyed AJ with his betrayal. At least Kevin had the decency to take his own life and avoid the certain painful death she knew AJ would exact upon him. No, AJ would have to have that on her conscience too.

"No, I'm afraid I have to work. Unlike your boss, it seems. If she calls in, would you tell her to call me? It's important."

"Did you try her cell?"

"I did and she's not answering."

"Oh dear."

That didn't sound good. "Do you know something I don't?"

"Oh, no. I didn't mean to sound rash or anything. I was just worrying aloud. You know how us old women like to worry. I think we should teach classes in it at the university since we're such experts in it."

Maggie laughed trying to lighten the mood. She was hiding something and Clarissa knew it. Noticing the time she realized she didn't have time to quiz the woman.

"Well, thanks Maggie. Have a good evening and tell your husband hello for me."

"Will do and don't worry, I'm sure AJ is fine. She'll be waiting for you when you get home."

"You're right of course. Have a good evening."

"Bye now."

Clarissa was worried. It wasn't normal for no one to know where AJ was. Her last hope was Selene. She doubted they'd kissed and made-up, but they did keep in contact.

Punching a button, her phone speed dialed Selene.

"Hello, Clarissa."

"Selene, have you talked to AJ today?"

"No, why?"

"I can't find her and I have a little…oh I'm sure it's nothing. If you talk to her could you tell her to call me?" Clarissa noticed the time and rushed past the niceties of the conversation. "Thanks."

Before Selene could say anything, Clarissa hung up and dashed to her class. The rule was, if a student was late said student had to sing their favorite nursery rhyme, and Clarissa wasn't going to be called out by her students for being late.

Chapter Twelve

Alexandra, you look wonderful. How long has it been?" Butch sauntered into the room looking like he had stepped out of a fifties movie: velvet slippers, a smoking jacket, fingering a cigarette in a holder. He air kissed each cheek and then sat down in a huge wingback chair that almost swallowed the slight man. "You look fantastic, being a light walker suits you. Pretty soon you'll be tan and healthy looking. It's such a shame we can't get out and tan like we used to, I miss the sun's heat. So…what brings you to the coven?"

A smoke ring encircled AJ, who stood, still trying to take in the ridiculous outfit.

"Sit." Butch motioned toward a chair to his right facing the roaring fireplace. "What brings you all the way out here? Tell me you want to rejoin the coven. We could use someone like you in the coven, Alexandra. I hear you're doing drug research into a blood replacement."

"Well that's not exactly right, Butch. I've got a government contract for plasma, extracting it out of the blood and making it into powder form." AJ lied. She didn't want Butch getting any ideas for her new hyper-concentrated blood product. He could use it for his legions of vampires, giving them a normal appearance to the humans who might suspect they had a vampire in their midst. It didn't have the ability to make them light walkers, and AJ wasn't sure what had given her the ability, but she wasn't risking anything. "They use it in the field, by adding water they get a stabilizer for the patient until they can get them the real stuff. At least we're hoping it works out that way."

"Hmm, I thought Kevin had said something else. Guess I misunderstood."

Kevin had shared her work with the coven? What other secrets would she find out that Kevin had shared? At least he was dead and couldn't say anything counter to her assertions now.

"I didn't know Kevin was reporting back to the coven. How long had that been going on?" AJ was starting to get steamed at the possible implications of Kevin's betrayal.

"Alexandra don't be so paranoid. He was a friend. We shared many conversations about different things. You weren't the only thing we talked about, besides I didn't know your research was a secret."

"When you work with the government on research like this, it *is* secret. I could lose the contract if word leaked out and they thought I was sharing information."

"Ah, I see. Well your secret is safe with me." He crossed his heart and held up three fingers emulating the scout code. "On my honor."

"I appreciate that, Butch. Now can we get to the reason I'm here?"

"Oh of course, where are my manners?" At the snap of his fingers an attendant appeared with two glasses filled with a red liquid on a serving platter. He presented it first to AJ and she hesitantly took a glass. She hadn't had real blood in years—with the exception of feeding off Clarissa in a sexual frenzy when they made love—but she wasn't sure she could drink it like this.

Butch lifted his glass in salute. "To your health and continued success, AJ."

"To the coven and your leadership, may you never waver about doing the right thing."

"Touché."

Lifting his glass, he slurped at the thick liquid. The action made AJ want to throw-up, setting the glass on the table she cringed thinking about how Butch had acquired the vampire lifesaving liquid. It was something that wasn't discussed in proper circles, but rumors swirled about how the coven *farmed* humans for their blood. It wasn't as bad as it sounded. The humans were paid for their fluids, but it was better than the barbaric way many still did it, often killing the human. The newbies resorted to killing their lunch, while the more sophisticated left them with little more than a few puncture marks and no memory of how they acquired them.

Pulling herself back to the present, she studied Butch as he devoured the liquid. Clearly, Butch was consuming more that his body required for survival. His exaggerated gut and body spoke volumes, but she didn't take him lightly even if he looked like a heart attack waiting to happen.

"I'm looking for some help with a problem, Butch."

"Hmm," he said lifting his finger to pudgy lips. "What would that problem be? Better yet, *whom* would that problem be?"

"I think you mean *who*."

"Who, whom, whatever. The result is still the same. I can't help, Alexandra."

"AJ."

"Whatever, Alexandra, AJ it's all the same person. I still can't help you. De Marcus is gone from the coven." He flitted his hand around as if dismissing her. She wasn't going to be rid of that easily.

AJ stepped closer to tower over Butch. She'd had enough of his pompous routine. "I know you two were thick as thieves. He knows where all your dead bodies are buried and you're afraid he'll expose just how you came to be the High Lord of the fucking coven, but guess what? I don't care. I'd be doing us both a favor by eliminating him from our vocabulary. Tell me where he is and I'll leave, never to be seen or heard from again."

She leaned in and Butch backpedaled in a failed attempt to escape. Their history kept him focused on her and on alert. AJ had almost killed him once and if he didn't come clean with the information he had on De Marcus, she might actually do it this time.

He straightened and tried to reassert his dominance by stepping forward and going nose to nose with AJ. She took another step forward. Butch slipped around her and placed his empty glass on the table. He moved to rest his elbows on the top edge of his wingback chair, creating a barrier between them. AJ smiled and sat casually on the sofa, waiting for his answer.

"Would you like a tour of the place?" Butch said, trying to work a diversion.

She glanced at her watch. "It seems I don't have time for the grand tour, Butch. I'm having dinner with my wife in a few hours."

"I'd love for you to see what we've done with the art collection. Thanks to you we have a few stunning pieces. I thought you might like to visit them for old time's sake."

Butch started toward the open doors to her left, leaving no room for discussion. Either she went along or went home to Clarissa. Leaving her mission incomplete was unacceptable. She wasn't ready to let Butch off the hook quite yet. The fact that he was taking her to gloat over *her* art collection was like adding salt to an open wound, but it would only sting for a little while.

"Fine."

He clapped his hands together and squealed with delight. No man should act like that, especially one who was in his position. AJ rolled her eyes as she followed him deeper into the bunker. Filing past one door and then another until they were almost at the end of the hall concerned AJ. The fact that no one was around gave her an uneasy feeling that something wasn't quite right.

"Here we are," Butch said rather loudly.

Light barely peeked out from the doorway as Butch entered. A crushing blow dropped AJ to her knees and then there was nothing but total darkness.

⁂

Selene jerked the phone from her ear in surprise. Clarissa wasn't usually rude, but something had her rushed. Dialing her back, Selene waited only to get her voice mail.

"Hey, it's just me. You hung up so fast that I didn't have time to ask what's going on. Call me back."

Selene had a feeling she knew what was wrong, but it wasn't her place to tell Clarissa that AJ was probably at the coven. There was something else in her voice though, fear, panic or…

She checked her watch. *Class.* If she was right, Clarissa's night class was just starting which would explain her hurry to hang up, but not the fear in her voice. Grabbing her jacket she slung it on, patted her chest to make sure her weapons were still in place and rushed to the door. It wouldn't take but a few minutes to get to the campus and then she could put her own concerns to rest.

Sliding into her low-slung black sports car, she cranked the music. The head banging tunes would drown out her thoughts. Her demons called her out when she was alone. There was no exorcising them. Since her family's death the demons were a constant reminder of why she did what she did—dealt death to those that deserved it. Only now she was paid for what she had taken pleasure in doing before. Before she could walk in the light.

The drive to the campus was too short. Sitting in her car, she let the music vibrate through the speakers into the doors and up through the floor. She kept the windows rolled up, and the world at bay. Suddenly, she wondered what Doctor Francesca Swartz was doing right at that moment. The doctor's shock of platinum blond hair and fair skin had instantly made Selene think vampire, but the warm pulse thrumming through her body alerted Selene that she was all human, and a scared one at that. But was she really scared? Doctor Swartz tensed when she walked in unannounced on Selene's meeting with AJ. A subtle reaction, however, Selene had picked up on the quickening pulse, the dilated eyes and the jagged breath Doctor Swartz drew when they made brief eye contact. Unfortunately, Selene wasn't as good at hiding her emotions when someone like AJ was around. AJ had honed in on her own visceral response like a hawk eyeing dinner. Doctor Swartz intrigued Selene and she would have to think of a way to see the good doctor, even if the excuse was for a brief cup of coffee. She'd better start drinking coffee if her stomach was going to handle the acidic liquid.

Jumping out of her car, she turned her attention back to the reason she was at the university, Clarissa. Selene jogged to the hallway where Clarissa's class was in session. She stood outside the door and listened as Clarissa lectured on how culture affected literature. Her voice steady but reserved, at least that's what Selene heard. Something was definitely up. Clarissa loved teaching. She had the gift of inspiration. Her students loved her and she loved them, genuinely loved them. They would go all out for the Renaissance Ball, held by the literature club every year. Selene had almost killed De Marcus at that same ball last year. If it hadn't been for that damned teacher he used to get to Clarissa, she would have one more on her kill list. Fate had its way of waving its boney fingers at her, flipping her the bird more times that she could count. No matter. She would get De Marcus if it killed her and that wasn't going to happen, not in this lifetime. Selene giggled at the thought.

"Okay class, meet back in fifteen minutes. When we get back we'll discuss how religion impacts literature."

The groan echoed out to the hallway. Students filed out the door and past Selene in the direction of the coffee klatch at the end of the hall. Clarissa walked past Selene too, not even giving her a glance. Tapping her on the shoulder earned Selene a squeal and a slap.

"What the–"

"Whoa, students," Selene said, pointing to the last few to exit the class.

"What are you doing here?"

"You called, I came." Selene sniffed the air, looked around and sniffed again. "Who is that?"

"You smell it too, huh?"

"Who?" Selene narrowed her eyes and peered down the hall searching for whomever the scent belonged to, but she couldn't pinpoint anyone.

Clarissa grabbed Selene's hand and led her down to her office, slamming the door behind them.

"Fuck, I'm scared shitless."

"What happened? Did someone touch you? Threaten you? If so, I'll kill them."

"That's just it. He was nice, too nice."

"Who was too nice?" Selene stood and tugged at the corner of the drapes, just enough to peek down the hall at the throng of students talking. Nothing, or should she say no one, out of the ordinary stood out. The giggling banter of young girls assaulted her ears, so she stepped away from the door hoping to avoid any more torture. "So who's this vamp?"

"I have no idea. He just showed up, taking Carol's place with some lame excuse that she had a family emergency."

"Maybe he's telling the truth?"

"Doubtful, Carol's dad is dead."

"Hmm."

"Have you talked to AJ? I really need to speak to her now." Clarissa sat behind her desk and worried a slip of paper and then wadded it up, throwing it in the trash with a sweeping arc.

"No, sorry. Maybe I can help. Where is this douche?" Selene stood and made a show of pushing up the sleeves of her jacket and walking to the door. Stopping, she looked over at her shoulder to Clarissa, hoping she wouldn't need to convince her that the guy only needed a good tongue-lashing.

Clarissa shuffled a few articles on her desk trying to appear busy, but Selene wasn't leaving without making sure Clarissa was safe. AJ wouldn't let her live if anything happened to Clarissa and she could've prevented it.

"I'm probably just over reacting. Don't pay any attention to me, Selene." Clarissa gave a half-hearted smile that didn't reach her eyes.

A sensation flooded through Selene, a feeling of dread perhaps. Clarissa's wide eyes told Selene she felt it, too. She opened the door and jerked the man walking past inside. In the next instant, she threw him on the sofa and straddled him.

"Is this him?"

Silence.

"Is this him?" Selene waited, hoping for confirmation before she did something someone would regret. Fear washed off Clarissa in waves and was all Selene needed. Her body took over before her mind could control it. Nails lengthened, her fangs dropped with a pop and she could feel her saliva glands start to overproduce, a signal she was ready to feed.

"Who the fuck are you?" Selene's voice dropped to a deadly level, whispering near his ear. She inhaled his scent as she leaned in closer to his neck. She could smell his last feeding as the blood boiled just below the surface of his skin. He was so young. He hadn't harnessed the ability to control his emotions and

Selene fed off that kind of aggression.

"Get off me," he said trying to angle himself from under Selene.

She only tightened her thighs, holding him under her.

"Look, obviously you don't know who I am, so take some advice, answer the question and I might let you live…" Holding his throat with one hand, she reached behind her and pulled a mat black dagger from its sheath. Pressing the thin chrome tip against his jugular she waited for it to pierce the skin releasing a drop or two of blood. Knowing the smell would send her further over the edge she resisted. "Or don't. Makes no matter to me."

Selene

"Clarissa, leave and you can say you don't know what happened to Mister Happy here."

Selene.

Clarissa's didn't have to give voice to her fear, Selene could read her mind, but it didn't matter. Out of the corner of her eye she saw Clarissa turn away, obviously not wanting to witness what was about to happen.

"So where were we? Aww yes, now where are your manners? You were about to introduce yourself. Weren't you?"

"Fuck you."

"Well, I have some bad news, you're not my type," Selene said rather casually. "Now see, you really don't know me. I like mine soft, with sexy curves and big red lips. Kind of like Clarissa over there, so that brings me back to my question. Why are you following Clarissa?"

"I'm the new substitute for Carol–" Selene

clamped down further on his throat. "…while she's out on emergency leave."

"Now you're lying. Carol's parents are both dead. Try again." Selene remembered a conversation between Clarissa and Carol when her job was Clarissa's safety.

Squeezing harder she closed her eyes and felt a sense of tranquility take over. His blood rushing past her fingers signaled a meal waiting just beneath grip. If his heart continued at its frantic pace, he might have a heart attack. That would solve the problem, but give her no answers. She relaxed her grip slightly, hoping he would see it as reluctance on her part to kill him. Selene liked playing cat and mouse with a prospective victim. The chase excited her, trying to out think her opponent had its merits and kept her sharp.

The vibrating fluorescent lights started to hurt her eyes. She was in hunt mode and her sensitivity to light and sound were heightened.

Turn off the lights.

Selene!

Leave now, Clarissa. I don't want you to be a part of this. Lock the door on your way out.

Her command left no room for resistance. Clarissa's haggard sigh, followed by footsteps and click of the lights showed her acquiescence to the situation. Selene didn't want Clarissa exposed to the impending death of this coward who was clearly only here to hurt Clarissa. Obviously, he hadn't counted on Selene and whoever sent him hadn't alerted him to the possibility of her presence. No, they had probably sent the young blood out to do their bidding without explanation, but a promise from a master would make any newling act like a loving puppy and do his bidding.

The sudden darkness added to the terror her victim experienced. Sweat started to bead on his top lip, another few slipping down his throat. She could almost taste his salty skin just before her teeth broke the surface to the delicate copper taste that would coat her throat. She tried to sweep his mind, but he was a young vampire who couldn't hide his fear. All she could see in her mind's eye was a chaos of thoughts, images flashing through his mind.

"Fuck off."

"Do you kiss your mother with that mouth? Oh, I suspect your mother is long dead isn't she?" Selene could feel the man under her trying to change. She squeezed his neck tighter. "Let me be frank, you're going to die tonight and you can either go with a clean conscience to meet your maker or you can carry all this baggage with you to the pearly gates. Makes no difference to me."

His eyes started to bulge as she squeezed the jugular smooth as it filled with the blood that wasn't making it past her grip. She flicked the tip of her blade and let loose a few droplets that dripped down his neck. She flicked her tongue up the drips catching them before they stained his shirt collar. Her mouth salivating, she plunged her fangs into the beckoning invitation. A long pull and her mouth filled with his essence. Pulling her head back, she stared into eyes ready to roll back into submission.

"Now, who sent you?" She licked the holes on his neck whispering again. "Tell me and I'll might let you live, don't and you'll surely die."

It had been at least a year since her last feeding on a person. Her body jerked and her mind reeled from the sudden infusion of raw human blood. It was almost orgasmic the way it sent spikes through her body. Her clit stiffened and wetness spread between her legs. A blood lust would set in after this and she knew what that meant. She'd be in need of a sexual partner.

"Butch."

"Hmm?" she hummed, her mind swimming in endorphins. Had she heard him right? The fucking high lord himself was sending someone to kill Clarissa. Why?

"Why would Van der Plume send someone to kill, Clarissa? You're a liar." Shocked at the revelation, she squeezed his neck tighter. Blood oozed from the puncture marks on his neck. While there was no love lost between the two, Butch didn't seem to have the balls or even the need to kill Clarissa. De Marcus, yes, Van der Plume, no.

"Why?"

"He has a plan to bring the coven back together and Alexandra and Clarissa are fucking with that plan. That's all I know." He croaked his answer past her grip.

Biting him again, she swallowed another mouthful or two and then pulled off his neck. Draining him almost to the point of death would keep him compliant and weak, but it would have the opposite effect on Selene. She would be unstoppable for the next few hours. Her mind raced in directions that were even fearful for her.

"How does Alexandra fit into all of this?" She knew, but needed him to confirm what she was afraid had already happened.

"She's at the coven as we speak. He's got a plan for her and—"

His head dropped back into unconsciousness. He'd been drained too far and would be in a coma like state for at least a few days until his body recovered enough to produce enough blood to sustain life. At least now he wasn't a threat to Clarissa, but Selene wasn't through with him yet.

Fuck.

Selene knew AJ had planned to visit the coven today. Remembering the last time they talked it was clear he was beyond reason. He wasn't one to do his own dirty work; this guy was evidence of that fact. She suspected whatever Butch had planned would involve more guys like this one. Drones who did their master's bidding.

"Selene?"

"Clarissa. Come in but don't turn the lights on. Do you have anything to clean this guy up with? I don't want to carry him out of here with a bloody neck."

"Oh my god, did you kill him?"

"Lucky for him, no."

Selene wished she had. Now she had to worry about where she would put him for safekeeping. The club was her only option. Jax would keep an eye on him and knew what to do when he came around. She needed to make her way to the coven and save AJ, if it wasn't too late.

Chapter Thirteen

Francesca wished she had passed on Dorothy's taunts, but now she would have to either pay-up or put-up with the spanking. She hadn't told anyone about the bet and she hoped Dorothy didn't either. Francesca also hadn't told Dorothy when she would fulfill her part of the bet. Dorothy gave her a month, but she wanted to get this over as soon as possible. It was bad enough that it was the only thing occupying her mind lately.

According to the paperwork she would be anonymous to the mistress and the patrons. Francesca marked what she absolutely wouldn't do and marked what she would consider. She even had to write down her safe word so that there was no mistaking what it was. The attendant had passed her the clothing she requested and tied her up. Then she informed Francesca that her mistress would be in to "discipline" her.

They agreed that proof would be a few strategically placed lash marks upon which Dorothy would pay the hundred dollars. If Dorothy didn't do it then she owed Francesca two hundred dollars. How could she pass up the chance at two hundred buck for a few minutes of *torture*?

"Hey boss, whatcha got there?" Jax tossed his head in the direction of the body slung over Selene's shoulder.

"A problem."

Selene was thankful Marshall didn't weigh more than his slight little frame could carry. Clarissa told her that his name was Marshall. No last name, just Marshall. She didn't have the heart to tell her what Marshall had relayed before he slipped into unconsciousness. It would freak her out even more if she thought AJ was at the coven, let alone in danger. Now Selene had two more problems besides confirming AJ's location. Her feeding frenzy had created a situation needing immediate attention and the man slung across her back had to be restrained and kept under guard.

"Want me to take care of your *problem*?"

"I'll put him in one of the rooms. I don't think he's a day walker so a room with some light filtering in will keep him down."

"I'm glad you're back, I have a newbie client in need of a mistress."

Selene stopped dead in her tracks. Did she hear him right? Did he solve her blood lust problem without knowing it? No. In her current condition, she could hurt someone. She'd have to pass on this *little* fix. Newbie night was turning out to be a bigger pain in the ass than she had hoped. It opened up a whole new clientele that had unfortunately read to many mommy porn books. But pain was a color and that color was green, money green and her business was flush with green.

"I don't think that's a good idea right now. Find someone else, Jax."

"She wants a woman, and all the other Doms are busy with clients. I can send her home and tell her to come back another time. No problem."

Shit, word of mouth was either the best business promoter or the worst thing for a business. One unsatisfied customer wouldn't kill her, but she didn't like the thought that someone would badmouth the Dungeon, either.

"No…let me dump this piece of shit in a room and cleanup. How long has she been waiting?"

"She just signed in and got situated in a room."

"All right, He's going in the basement room. Keep the camera live on him. He won't be coming around anytime soon, but I don't want him finding a way out and running back to his master. Got it?"

"You got it."

"Don't touch him, Jax."

Jax threw up his hands. "Why would you even think I would lay a hand on a hair on his head? I'm shocked, Selene." His mock indignation made her want to slap him silly.

"I mean it, Jax. I need him to tell me what's going on at the coven and he can't do that if he's dead."

Selene humped down the stairs and unceremoniously dumped her cargo on the cement floor. Pulling out her phone, she snapped a picture for later identification, but for now she had a job to do. She tossed a light on and double locked the door without even a second glance and made her way back upstairs. She'd had enough drama for the night and needed to get her head screwed on right if she was about to work.

Selene changed and made her way to the room where her client awaited her introduction into the world of bondage. Flipping through the paperwork she made sure all the T's were crossed and the I's dotted before she looked through the peep hole. It would take all she had to control her visceral response to the bondage session, but if she were lucky it would help her work through the sexual urgency coursing through her body.

Looking in she froze. There was no way she was going into that room.

Walking back to the front she found Jax standing at the bar chatting with a woman who looked as if she belonged in a steampunk novel than a bondage club. Why did some people insist on dressing up when coming to the Dungeon? She would never understand the urge of some people to get trussed up, strapped around and sheathed in whatever the flavor of the day was for a night of twisted fetish pleasure. Sure, she knew there was a whole culture surrounding the bondage theme. It just wasn't her thing. She had no idea why she was so judgmental of those that wanted to be part of that experience. They were who they were, she guessed.

"Jax can I speak to you for a minute?"

"What's up boss?"

"I can't do this client."

Jax shot her a puzzled look and then smiled. "No problem, boss. I'll take care of it."

Selene grabbed his bicep, stopping him from coming around the bar. "No, I don't want you taking care of *it*. Who's on tonight?"

Jax ticked off names on his fingers, all which under any other circumstances would be capable of giving a newbie their first taste of BDSM. Only this client was different, this client was the woman Selene had just been engaged in daydreaming about.

Fuck me, she muttered to herself. She couldn't trust anyone else with this woman. If anything went wrong she'd never forgive herself. What could go wrong? Her Dom's did this for a living, they wouldn't be here if they couldn't control themselves. A pang of jealousy charged through her body at the thought of someone else in charge of Francesca's first fetish experience.

"Forget it, I'll take her."

❧❧❧❧

Francesca heard the door to the private room open and then shut.

"Your safe word is tiger? Interesting," said a voice she could barely hear, her heart was beating so loudly in her ears. She felt a hand slowly trail around her mid-section, ending on her back. "Ready?"

"Yes Mistress," she whispered as she lowered her head.

"Don't be scared. I won't hurt you." The voice tried to reassure her, but she felt like she'd suddenly made a mistake. She tried to control her anxiety with a deep breath and then pushed it out through pursed lips. Francesca was always in control in her life. She controlled her environment even when she did nothing, because wasn't doing nothing still a control mechanism? Her mind raced as she heard something being dropped on the bench along the wall. Francesca turned towards the noise. She couldn't quite make out what was happening, but the sound of a metal chain, or at least she thought it was a metal chain, drew closer. Now she'd wished she had more clothing on.

In fact, flannel pajamas sounded good right about now, the exact opposite of what she had on, or barely had on. Francesca had decided that if she wanted to experience the total scene she needed to be open what she had witnessed at the Dungeon the night before. The woman on stage wore only a bustier and panties and had sent a surge of electricity through her. She looked…sexy. Francesca never felt sexy, but tonight she wanted to feel it, live it. She would never see the dominatrix again, she had told herself repeatedly as she dressed in her outfit for the night. That alone helped her cinch up the laces of the bustier. Anonymity, complete and total anonymity, was promised in the paperwork. That, and a stupid bet with Dorothy were the only ways she had convinced herself to sign up for this experience.

"You've picked an interesting outfit for tonight. Did you decide on this little leather number?"

Francesca nodded.

"It's very flattering on you."

Did she just imply I was sexy?

Francesca felt something warm touch her nipples and then they were pulled and squeezed. A pinch on her nipples almost made her knees buckle, the painful pressure sweet in a way she hadn't expected. Cold metal swayed against her chest as the chain was pulled and released, slapping her.

Hmm, she groaned.

"Are you all right?" A warm whisper caressed her ear.

"Yes."

"Yes, *ma'am*. You will always address me as ma'am or mistress. Understand?" The voice firm, continued to breath in her ear as the chain was pulled lightly at first.

"Yes…" A tug on the chain stopped her briefly. "Ma'am."

"Good girl."

Francesca felt a burst of wind on her back as she heard the swishing of the flogger being moved back and forth. *SLAP*, small strokes landed on her back and then more as the dominatrix worked the leather instrument back and forth.

"Is that too hard?"

"No." A harder slap made her wince, not in pain but something different, a tingle of sorts.

"No, Mistress."

"That's better," the woman said as she moved to the front of Francesca.

Slowly, she felt the flogger worked around her body. The sting of the flogging was starting to send tremors through her body. She had been told that endorphins would be released when she was flogged and it was clear the mistress knew the exact amount of pain it would take to release them. She felt her nipples harden against the clamps, sending a painful jolt through her. A sudden gasp and the mistress stopped her flogging.

"Are you all right?"

Cool hands ran down the long welts the flogger had left behind.

"Yes, Mistress," Francesca said. She felt the woman move into her.

Francesca pushed against the hand that rested on her hip, suddenly embarrassed that she was wishing for a more intimate contact. Automatically, she turned into the hand and shifted towards the mistress. Her body was on a slow burn that wanted to be fully ignited. *It's the endorphins*, she told herself. Her rational mind tried to take over but her body was on a different path. One of sexual urgency and release.

Without warning the mistress cupped her pubic bone and let her fingers slowly stroke her clit.

"You like this don't you? I can tell by the way you're breathing and..." She fingered the fabric barrier. "You're wet. Very wet."

Francesca felt herself getting wetter the longer the stroking went on. The slow dance of the mistress's fingers almost made her come, but she was in control of her body, wasn't she?

"Would you like to come? I know what you're thinking. You think you're a nasty girl for liking this aren't you?"

When an answer did come, the mistress gradually released the pressure on a nipple clamp and then reapplied it.

"OOO. Yes Mistress please,"

"Please, what?"

"Please, I...I...need to come. If you keep stroking me I'll come."

"Then answer my question?" The mistress slid a tongue around Francesca's ear lobe as she continued to stroke her.

"Yes, I'm ashamed I've liked this too much."

"Well don't be, enjoy what your body likes. Leave the taboos outside and you'll enjoy yourself more." The mistress slipped two fingers inside Francesca and continued to play with the nipple clamps.

"Are you ready Francesca?" Francesca groaned, feeling a tug on the chain that tethered her to the bondage experience.

"Yes, mistress."

"Good, come for me." The mistress said, withdrawing her fingers.

Francesca's body jerked and spasmed in orgasm. The ecstasy intensified as the mistress started to flog her again. Each lash marking her body as if the mistress was claiming it as her own. The nipple clamps were released sending spikes of pain, further stimulating her clit. A cool hand caressed one nipple and a warm tongue caressed the other as she her body shuddered. She felt a warm body behind her, hands claiming her, as the mistress caressed her stomach and thighs, stopping only briefly to pull the binding from her eyes.

Francesca remained still as her eyes adjusted to the dim light of the room. She wanted to see the woman who had opened a new door in her life, but was frightened to move without receiving permission.

"Our session is over, Francesca." The mistress said, releasing her.

Francesca waited for further instructions and then it registered she called her by name. *Francesca.* She waited. Nothing followed, so she slowly turned just in time to catch a glimpse her mistress as she left.

Selene.

Chapter Fourteen

AJ barely opened her eyes. She searched for movement in the darkness her but saw nothing in the stark room. Her head throbbed with each push of blood through her veins. Reaching back, she touched the knot resulting from whatever or whoever had hit her from behind. Lying still, she listened for any clue that might tell her where she was. She *was* sure she was still in the coven, but where? What was Butch's reason for having her cold-cocked? Sitting up almost made her faint as the blood rushed from her head. Nausea washed over her and bile etched its way up her throat.

"Christ," she whispered. Leaning against the cold cement wall, she shivered. The temperature was cold enough to be a beef locker and she rubbed her arms to warm her cramping muscles. Her messenger bag was gone, along with her phone, and keys. Tapping her slacks she felt the small tin of the new blood capsules she had stuck in her pocket when she left the office, nested safely away from prying eyes. Orienting herself in what seemed to be her prison she saw only a sliver of light slicing beneath the bottom of the door. Walking over to examine the surface, she slid her hand along the smooth metal, finding no door handle. Her fingertips grazed a small square door in the middle of the door. Hinges at the bottom alerted her that at least it could be opened. Fingering the hinge, she bent closer and studied the way it was made. Without anything to use to pry it, she doubted she could open it. Two huge hinges hung the larger door in its frame.

Walking her way along the walls, she ran her hands over them and counted out the length of each. Smooth, cold and nothing. No marks, no holes, no windows. A pang of anxiety threaded through her. Nobody knew where she was and Clarissa wouldn't miss her for hours. How long had she been out? She rubbed her wrist and felt her watch. They hadn't taken it. She'd been out for two hours. Another hour and Clarissa would be home. *God, if I'd only left a note.* AJ wished she'd taken Selene's advice now.

AJ sat back down on the metal bed. What was Butch up to? What game was he playing and when did she get a chance to make a move?

Several sets of heavy footsteps echoed down the hall and drew closer. Metal scraped against metal and the door opened, flooding the cell with light.

"Well Alexandra, I see you're awake–"

"What the fuck is going on, Butch?" AJ stood, but before she could move closer two men stepped into the cell with guns drawn. "Isn't that a little excessive, even for you?"

"Alexandra, Alexandra…do you really think I've lived this long being careless around people like you?"

"What do you mean people like me?"

"It's no secret you want me dead, Alexandra. I'm just surprised you had the nerve to show up here acting so innocent." Butch leaned against the door and leered at AJ.

"What the hell are you talking about? I came here hoping you'd see reason and help me get De Marcus." AJ felt her temper getting the best of her.

Watching the men who stepped closer, she knew the guns wouldn't kill her, but it would take her down long enough for Butch to either drain her or cut her head off, killing her either way.

"He said you'd say that." Butch sipped from the cup he carried into the room. AJ could smell the coagulating blood and she wanted to wretch.

"He, who?"

"De Marcus."

Butch smiled a sickening sweet smile that made AJ want to puke. De Marcus. It figured he was behind Butch's hysteria about protecting the coven against her. What other poison had De Marcus planted in Butch's demented mind? AJ had suspected Butch was losing his marbles decades ago, but as long as he had left her alone she didn't care if the bastard went bat-shit crazy holed up in the coven. The life of a vampire had a bloody secret no one wanted to talk about, mental illness. Living so long sometimes wore on those not ready for it. Changes in culture, times, and even countries could start to drive someone mad. AJ had seen it before, the dementia-like state some vampires lapsed into replaced their ability to think and react clearly. The weakest reverted back to their early days of feeding frenzies and violence. If they were lucky someone put them down quickly before they made a mess of things. AJ had heard of a group of vampires that had formed to exterminate the mentally ill. It was an ugly thing to have to do, but she applauded their efforts to keep the bloodlines clean. Often times these rogue vampires turned drug dealers, gang bangers and other nefarious types that would keep them supplied with fresh meat. The consequence of these gangs was that they were more dangerous than the mental patient who turned them. Clearly, he was past crazy and on his way to being a raving lunatic with the help of someone even more maniacal than himself.

"You've got to be kidding me, Butch. Answer me this, why would I come here if I wanted to kill you?" AJ knew reasoning with someone like Butch was hopeless, but she needed to try and save her life. "I could wait until you were out at night somewhere alone, all by yourself and slit your throat."

"See, I knew you wanted to kill me. I'm just smarter than you, admit it AJ." Butch stepped back as AJ swung for him.

"You stupid bastard—" She took a gun butt to her stomach and gutted out the rest, "You're being played for a fool."

Falling to her knees she dry heaved, gasping for breath. She'd kill Butch just for the pleasure of watching the life seep out of his eyes. There was no way he was going to leave the coven alive.

"Alexandra, one would think you would've learned your lesson by now." A deep voice boomed in the room.

De Marcus.

Why wasn't she surprised? He'd made it clear that Clarissa was his and that she was the only thing standing in his way of having her. Now she'd finally come face-to-face with the bastard.

"De Marcus, still the same pompous ass you were way back when?" She stared up into the shadow that blocked the light seeping in behind him. She couldn't see his face, but she didn't need to, his image was burned into her retinas. The only thing that would exorcise that would be to kill the bastard.

"Still the bitch I remember. Looks like things aren't working out too well for you, now are they?" Shoe leather tried to make contact with AJ's face but she shifted to her side easily enough, grabbing his loafer and pulling him down to the floor. With lightning quick reflexes, she bit his ankle and sucked. The taste of his putrefied blood almost made her throw it back up, but she held on as long as she could before rolling him under the weight of her body. Straddling him, she landed two good punches before she was wrestled off him.

"You fucking bitch you're going to pay for that, you know," he growled, rubbing his ankle and baring his fangs. As he moved closer AJ struggled to break free of the guards grip. Her arms were wrenched behind her back and the guards forced her forward, exposing her neck to the sharp tips of De Marcus' bite. She felt him sink his fangs into her neck, his cold lips wrapping around creating a suction that made her ill. She started to gag, just his touch her made her want to vomit. Before she could protest, De Marcus' head was yanked off her neck.

"Off, De Marcus. We need her if we're going to get Clarissa and Selene."

The pain as his fangs tried to stay anchored, nearly ripping her flesh made her scream out in pain.

"You fucking bastard. I'll make you pay for that."

"Relax, Alexandra. You'll live for now."

The fact that he kept calling her by her old name was an irritant she could ignore, but Butch's droll responses to the threat at hand was starting to grate on her. He clearly didn't see the way De Marcus was manipulating him. De Marcus obviously had him so twisted, the truth was something that hung out on the periphery if his mind, just out of reach.

The smell of coppery blood permeated the room. The guards' visceral reaction was evident as they tried to control their amped up bodies from changing. Sweat beaded on their faces as AJ moved into a corner of the room. From her vantage point she could see the potential explosion and like a dog, backed into a corner. She started to morph into a form she hadn't taken in a year, not since she'd been attacked out on a running trail in the park. Her guts churned as De Marcus' blood worked its way through her. Her fingers cracked, her nails lengthened and she squeezed her body tight, trying to control her urge to fight back.

"Relax," Butch said through an inappropriate laugh. "Everyone calm down. Boys, back out and leave us. I think I can handle Ms. Locke."

Bastard!

"Alexandra, we're going to keep you here for a few days, just until we have what we want." Butch's maniacal smile creased his forever-young face.

"And what is that?" She knew the answer, but playing dumb might help.

"Selene."

"And Clarissa," De Marcus added. "Don't forget I want what's mine. She belongs to me."

"Yes, yes, you'll have your precious Clarissa, De Marcus."

"Over my dead body," AJ said, standing. Sliding against the wall she tried to move closer to the duo. "I won't let you touch a hair on her head, you bastard."

"You won't be around to stop me. See with you in here, you won't be able to feed and if you don't feed, you die. So, how long would you say that will take

Butch? A week, maybe two?"

"Funny you should ask, my friend. If we help it along it could take a matter of days at the most." Butch snapped his fingers and two men carrying what looked to be medical equipment walked in and waited by the door.

"Don't do this, Butch. I'm warning you this could get ugly."

"Alexandra, you aren't exactly in a position to negotiate or give orders." Butch looked at the men and tossed his head towards AJ.

"I want that bitch to suffer, so don't drain her completely. I want her to feel death approaching, to contemplate what she's done to me and how her life will end. I want her body to be ravaged by the lack of blood, to feel the torture as it eats itself alive." De Marcus stuck his hands in his pants pockets and leaned against the cold cement wall.

"Oh don't worry, she'll suffer. A day or two, three at the most, if all goes as planned. That will give us time get to Selene and Clarissa before they start to worry and go bananas."

"Guards," Butch yelled. "Hold her down."

AJ had one chance and that was to bulldoze her way past the bulky men. Fully changed she growled, put her head down and ran towards the men. Surprise wasn't her friend. One of the men pulled a Taser and shot her. The electricity surged through her body, jerking her to a stop, flopping her to the floor. Her mind said fight, but her body could only writhe as the man held the trigger down for a continuous jolt.

"Okay, that's enough. She's down."

AJ felt the tingling in her muscles as the effects of the Taser wore off. It wouldn't kill her, but she'd feel it for a while. She searched the room, trying to fix on something to keep her mind focused. Nothing came into view but the brightness from the lights overhead. A poke in her arm made her grimace in pain and then she felt it. Her life's essence being drained from her. It was slow at first, like the first effects of a drug high, relaxing and mind altering, as her brain was slowly deprived of life. She tried to look down to see how much blood they'd taken but her head was held in place. De Marcus' face hovered over hers. She wanted to reach up to wipe the sneer off his face, but she could move.

"Okay, that's enough." Butch held two bags of blood over her for inspection. "This should do it. I'll be enjoying this later, Alexandra. So, while you're in here dying, I'll be drinking you. Poetic don't you think?"

"Fuu...f...fuck you," she rasped out. Her eyes could only follow his back as he left with the others. The slam of the door proof they were gone.

"How long do you think it will take?" A voice she didn't recognized asked.

"Not long, trust me. I've done this before. I want you to check on her in a few hours, maybe tomorrow and give us a progress report. We're going to find Clarissa. If Selene shows up, keep her busy until we return."

The voices faded away.

Chapter Fifteen

Clarissa pulled up to the entrance of her driveway, pushed the button for access, and pulled through the security gate. Watching it close in her rearview mirror, she looked around, searching for anything that might be out of place. She'd conditioned herself, at AJ's urging, to be more observant of her surroundings. Clarissa wasn't as bad as AJ who preferred to sit with her back to the wall in a restaurant and face the door. AJ was becoming paranoid and it worried Clarissa.

Darkness closed around her as she made her way up the driveway. It felt good to be home, in her space and surrounded by her things. She'd taken things to AJ's and AJ, please her heart, had never made her feel like a guest. In fact, she'd done the exact opposite the moment they'd found each other. Smiling, she remembered their first time together after finding each other again.

"Alexandra, please..." Clarissa's voice, heavy with desire, pleaded. "...I'm not sure that I can—"

AJ snapped out of her self-induced haze. "I'm sorry. I don't know what I was thinking." Trying to stand, AJ felt a hand push her back.

"Stop." Clarissa cupped AJ's face in her hands and steadied her. "I was going to say, I don't know if I can stop. I don't know if I want to stop." Translucent pools of green started to shift into a darker, urgent green.

Clarissa struggled with herself. Trying to maintain her composure, her body begged for release. "I've hurt you tonight and I'm the one that's sorry. I'm sorry for ever believing De Marcus, for believing that you'd hurt my family." A finger stopped Clarissa's lips, but she pulled it down and continued, "For never coming to find you. I've wasted all of these years with bitterness and anger, and thoughts of revenge."

Standing, AJ pulled Clarissa even tighter to her body, her lips next to her ear. "Listen to me. Every breath I share with you is a gift, one I don't want to take for granted. Tomorrow will take care of itself, so let's take tonight to explore and reacquaint ourselves with each other. Let me make love to you. Please?" AJ knew she sounded desperate, but it was all she had right now. The strong, independent woman was left at the ball. She had humbled herself to Clarissa in hopes of reconciling with her and she wasn't ashamed of it. But tomorrow she knew what she needed to do, so tonight she needed to right her world with Clarissa. She needed to show Clarissa she hadn't forgotten about her, that the monster Clarissa thought she was had never existed. Not then, not now and not ever.

AJ felt Clarissa wrap her legs around her waist, gently rocking her hips against AJ's rock hard abs underneath the sweatshirt. The walk to AJ's room was painstakingly slow and arduous. Each thrust against AJ's body was an exercise in patience. Grabbing Clarissa's ass AJ pulled her up and kissed her. AJ's tongue demanded entrance and wouldn't be denied. Feeling as if she would swallow Clarissa whole, AJ lowered her lips to the pulsing vein and started to caress the throbbing underneath. Moans had replaced the pleading and AJ tried to move faster, but spied the couch and decided to nestle Clarissa into its leathery palm. The bedroom would be for another time.

That moment, that one moment in time would replace all the hurt, the pain and the misery Clarissa had endured at the hands of De Marcus. Forgiveness had taken time, and AJ had given her every opportunity to leave in the months that followed. No pressure, no guilt, just plenty of time. A love like theirs couldn't be rushed, but it couldn't be forgotten either.

"Come on Nef, we're home. Well, we're at our other home," Clarissa said, pulling the kitty carrier out of the back seat. Clarissa flinched and covered her eyes when the security light picked up her movement and flashed on. AJ had them installed after Selene had killed the assassin who'd thought Clarissa was an easy target. The perimeter and the house were lined with lights and cameras, catching any action that might take place. The reassuring purr of Nefertiti always brought Clarissa back to reality and a quick smile. A serenity washed over Clarissa, as she pushed the door open and watched as Nefertiti regally exited her confined space. Arching and stretching and then brushing against her pant leg, before launching herself into the darkness beyond the driveway, Nefertiti was home.

"Don't run off, you might forget how to get home and I don't feel like coming to look for you silly girl." Clarissa keyed the lock and tossed her messenger bag on the bench in the mudroom. Flopping on the bench, she took a deep breath and leaned against the wall. The musty smell, laced with a hint of AJ's perfume, relaxed her further. Pushing into her slippers, she wandered into the kitchen, turning on the lights, ready to start dinner. Pushing her finger along the counter, feeling a fine layer of dust, another sign it had been a while since her last visit home.

"I need to give this place a thorough cleaning," she said to an empty house. The click of the swinging pet door signaled Nefertiti's return. Her cat dropped the gift of a dead mouse to the floor in front of her. Clarissa cringed, knowing she would have to dispose of it. AJ was nowhere to be found, yet. She could always wait until AJ arrived for dinner, but the dead rodent would unnerve her if it sat on the floor for much longer.

"Neeeefffff, come get your toy and put it away." Flicking lights on as she strolled through the house in search of her cat brought Clarissa a little more comfort until finally all the lights were on. "Nef?"

The house was exactly as she had left it. Dusty, but still in order. Nothing out of place, nothing disturbed. Why wouldn't it be? Clarissa's mind knew the answer to why, De Marcus was still out there, searching for her, she was sure. He wouldn't give up so easily and she knew the coven could possibly be covering for him would only bolstered him in his mission. She had no protection, a harem never did. They were always at the whim of their master to do his bidding. She was still his property, the fact that he hadn't claimed her in decades made no matter to the coven nor to a master. If he called, they had no choice but to respond. It was only a matter of time before it happened. Maybe that's why Clarissa never truly turned herself over to AJ. It was an unwritten law between them. AJ could do nothing to stop De Marcus, short of killing him, and he had proven elusive to the point of being almost invisible. He would show up when he wanted and not a minute before. Everything had been on his terms. He had turned her, she depended upon him for life and then it was all gone. Poof. A faked death had transformed her life, or so she thought. Then De Marcus was there, inserting his finger into her world and swirling it around, fucking things up.

"What did I do to deserve this life?" she said to an empty house.

Maybe wanting time away from AJ was her way of coming to terms that their life was not really in their control. He would come for her. Now that she knew he was alive, she was sure of it. Breaking away from AJ might be the best for both of them. It would be hard to push AJ away, especially now that they come so far, and knitted their lives back together. De Marcus had created quite a ruse with the story of how AJ had killed her family and he had saved her. He claimed he'd turned her to keep her safe from the *rabid* animal AJ had become when her family forbade her from seeing Clarissa. Oh, he was clever, so bold and yet with a flash of white she was his for eternity.

Spotting a bottle of wine on the counter, she pulled the cork and sniffed it. Her nose wrinkled at the slight hint of vinegar. Pouring it down the drain, she tossed the empty bottle into the trash and grabbed an unopened bottle from the rack in the island. She needed a drink to settle her nerves. She had a choice to make, leave AJ and wait for De Marcus to come for her, or…. There was no other choice, he would come and she would leave with him. It was the natural law of things. Better to break away now than to try and hang on, watching him kill her lover. She wasn't giving him too much credit and AJ not enough, just the opposite – she knew AJ would fight to the death for her. If AJ died, then what would she have to live for? Taking a sip of her red wine she knew the answer - she would have to do this so AJ could live. Looking down at her phone on the counter, with regret she pressed the off button. It would start tonight. No dinner, no phone calls, no contact between them. It was for AJ's own good.

Chapter Sixteen

Selene practically ran to her office, slammed the door shut and fell against it. Her transformation had started. Licking the blood from her lips, she still tasted Francesca. Pure, innocent, and a virgin. Fuck. She was untainted by another. She felt it instantly when the blood hit her tongue, bits of Francesca's life flashed in Selene's mind.

"Oh god." Selene slid down as she tried to control her body. Her blood was on fire, ravaging her mind with temptation of another taste of Francesca. Thoughts of Francesca tied up, her body giving Selene what she wanted, ran rampant in her mind. A virginal offering, and in the throes of a blood lust, what could be more dangerous for a vampire? She clenched her hands tighter, digging her nails into her palms, wishing the pain would help ease her desires.

A soft tap on the door jerked her from her thoughts.

"Selene?"

Francesca.

"Selene. I know it was you."

"You must go, Francesca." Selene sniffed the air like a dog in heat. She could smell Francesca, feel the throbbing of her blood as it coursed through her body. Her mind clouded with the vision of Francesca offering herself, bent over by her desire to explore Francesca's body—to taste her again—even if just a lick.

"Did I do something wrong?"

"No." *God please go.* Selene wanted to splinter the door and possess what her body wanted—no, needed.

"I wanted to tell you that…well…that what happened tonight was…"

Selene hung on every word drifting through the door. Her body responded when Francesca leaned against the door and pressed her lips to the seam and whispered, "Amazing."

Selene's mind was on fire. Without another thought she stood, whipped the door open and Francesca fell into her arms. Her lips claimed Francesca's as her hands ripped open her shirt, shredding it in the process. She hesitated a moment and then gratefully realized Francesca couldn't see her in her condition. Her office lights were off and the windows were wrapped in heavy drapery, blocking out even the slightest bit of sun or street lighting. Expecting resistance, she found none. It was the exact opposite. Francesca pushed herself into Selene's body. Her hands roamed trying to grasp at anything. She grabbed Francesca's wrists and pinned them behind her back. The last thing she needed was for Francesca to notice she was in the throes of changing. Her nails bit into wrists that acquiesced and relaxed, her lips found burgeoning breasts pushing toward her mouth. Francesca's low moan when she nipped at her nipple practically sent Selene spiraling out of control.

Moving Francesca toward her desk, she swept her arm across it, scattering everything to the floor. She laid Francesca on top and pulled at her jeans with such force the buttons closing the front went flying in all different directions. Frantic for contact, Selene fell to her knees and began to rub her face against the soft skin laid bare between Francesca's legs. Her lips rubbed against the wet, matted hair before parting it with her tongue. She couldn't get enough of Francesca. Dipping her tongue between velvety soft lips, she darted in and out of her opening. Fingers threaded through her hair urging her further as Francesca's hips began to work against her tongue. She was beyond help, beyond reason as she tumbled over the edge of darkness into ecstasy. There was no way she could slip her fingers into Francesca without hurting her, so she speared her harder with her tongue, the quivering of an orgasm starting as she continued.

If Francesca looked down she would see Selene for who she really was, and yet Selene knew something kept her from doing just that.

"Oh, oh, fuck me. Please fuck me."

Francesca's moans spurred her further. Grabbing her hips, Selene pulled her tight and bit the soft lip under her tongue. Blood seeped into her mouth as she lapped up the warmth. A gush of wetness coated her mouth as Francesca orgasmed and Selene broke through the thin barrier of skin tethering them together now. A thick warmth coated her tongue as Selene continued to coax another orgasm from Francesca, milking it gently before letting go of her self-control.

"Don't stop, please don't…"

Another wave crashed over them. Francesca held Selene's head against her as her body convulsed. Blood coated her tongue, its essence enthralling Selene.

Chapter Seventeen

AJ lay on the ground barely able to move. The bright lights only added to her pounding headache and nausea. Trying to move, she remembered the jolt of electricity that surged through her before she collapsed. Her fingers glided over the two protruding wires still attached to her. *The least they could have done was take these bitches out.* She pulled the hooked tips from her skin. Her rational mind tried to grasp what had just happened. They had drained her blood to a dangerously low level.

She was going to die.

Her emotional mind struggled to imagine how she would live long enough to kill Butch and De Marcus. The process of dying was underway. Her lips were stuck together, and her swollen tongue could barely move in her dry mouth. Trying to stand, she fell face down. *This can't be the way it ends.* She had to fight for Clarissa. Pulling herself slowly along the floor, she tried to make her way to the steel bed. Every pull was a drain on her already weak system. Her arms felt like lead as she crawled, arm over arm, reaching out for the edge of the steel frame.

A break, she just needed a few minutes to compose herself and rest. Blackness ebbed into her mind, threatening to take her down into its dark abyss. Memories of Clarissa floated towards her. Happier times in France made her smile. Clarissa had been so beautiful in her innocence. For AJ it had been love at first sight. Shaking her head, she refused to give in to the debilitating weakness preceding death. She needed to stay focused in this world.

"Clarissa needs me," she told herself, grasping for the edge of the bed.

Her fingertips clung to the edge as she curled legs under her body. If she could tuck them under her, she could possibly raise herself up. She struggled to grab more of the edge to pull herself onto the bed, when something in her pocket caught, preventing her from achieving her goal.

"Fuck." AJ tried to roll her body onto the bed. With half her body hanging off, she nearly fell back to the floor. Teetering on the edge, she held the wall for support. She closed her eyes. All she could think about was sleeping. Just a short rest, that's all she needed. Clarissa's face filled her mind.

"AJ get up."

"I can't, love. I'm too tired. Just let me rest for a moment. Then I'll get up."

"No. If you rest you'll die. Get up, Alexandra, now!"

"Love-"

"NOW."

"I'm trying."

"Your pocket."

"My pocket?"

AJ reached for the pocket that had caught on the edge of the bed and felt around. Something pushed against her leg and she tapped her slacks. Reaching in, she pulled something out. She tried to look at it but her vision was dimming due to the lack of blood. Drawing it closer, she recognized the small box of experimental capsules Dr. Swartz had given her during their meeting. Elation coursed through AJ. Someone was definitely looking out for her. She fumbled with the tightly hinged tin and suddenly the capsules went flying in all directions.

Fuck.

One, just one would help her. She felt around her in the darkness. Nothing Her head lolled back against the bed, her mind weary with impending death. She felt as if she would succumb at any moment. "Rest, I just need to rest for a minute," she whispered and closed her eyes.

❧ ❧ ❧ ❧

Francesca lay on the desk, the last orgasm still buzzing through her body. Selene knelt with her head resting against Francesca's leg, her hands clutching her breasts. Unthreading her fingers from Selene's hair, Francesca reached out to stroke one of Selene's hands. Selene jumped to her feet. Suddenly embarrassed, Francesca covered her breasts and sat up.

"I'm sorry, I don't know what came over me. I mean, I just—"

"No need to apologize," Selene said.

"Oh, I see. Well—"

"It's I who should be apologizing. I've lost my professionalism and let myself take advantage of your heightened state. Let me get you some clothing."

Francesca looked down to see her shirt torn to shreds and her jeans around her ankles. The darkness shrouded her blush. Embarrassed again, she jumped off the desk and pulled at her pants, wondering where her panties and bra ended up.

"Mind if I turn on a light?"

"As a matter of fact, I do. Sorry, I'm a little embarrassed and light would only add to it."

Selene's admission shocked her, but she had to agree, a little light on the situation would only compound her tenuous hold on reality. She'd never done anything like this before and couldn't explain her irrational behavior now.

"I understand. I should be going. I think I left my jacket and purse in the changing room. I'll..."

"Wait," Selene spoke so softly that Francesca almost didn't hear her.

"Yes?"

"Nothing, it's nothing. Again, please accept my apology for my behavior. I don't know what came over me."

Francesca wanted to comfort Selene, but she resisted the urge.

"Can you answer me one question?"

"If I can," Francesca said.

"Are you a virgin?"

A secret she had held close was suddenly in front of her, daring to be denied.

Chapter Eighteen

*H*elp!”

“What?”

“Help me, baby,” a voice called out to Clarissa.

Reaching into the darkness, Clarissa pushed towards the voice she could barely hear. Pushing her hand further into the shadows her fingertips brushed against something cold.

“Grab my hand,” Clarissa whispered. She squinted and tried to peer deeper into the abyss that spiraled into nothingness.

“Clarissa, I can't move. You've got to help me, baby.”

“AJ?” Clarissa edged closer, extending her body further. AJ needed her. “Grab my hand, AJ.”

“I'm trying, but I can't see you. Help...”

“AJ.”

Clarissa slipped over the edge, falling, her body tumbling into the darkness. She tensed and waited for the impact as she fell further and faster into the emptiness reaching for AJ. A thud on her chest made her gasp, jarring her awake.

“Neff...” She grabbed for the startled cat. She couldn't pull in enough air as she tried to kick her feet free of the blanket that had wound around her legs. Finally, she sat up, shoving it off. Clutching her chest she gulped in each lungful of air, trying not pass out from hyperventilating. With her head between her knees she finally was able to control herself, but her mind raced with worry. Connection with another vampire had its pluses and minuses. The plus - knowing what they were thinking, how they were feeling, the minus - knowing what they were thinking and how they were feeling. Clarissa took her dreams seriously. They'd shown her what her inner mind was sensing in the past. This time her dream was alerting her that AJ was in danger. Maybe she was just feeling guilty. Leaving AJ wasn't easy, not when she had just found her, but De Marcus would come calling any day and it would be over for them.

Clarissa rubbed the sleep from her eyes and looked around trying to re-familiarize herself with surroundings she hadn't been at in a while. She was used to the hum of AJ's house that always seemed to be full of energy of some type, but an eerie quiet filled her house. She'd been gone so long that she hardly recognized the solace of the country. She'd become used to the speed and rhythm of the city. The constant noise that enveloped them anytime they went out, the crush of people that mingled on the street from sun up to the red haze of dusk was a constant.

Her mind quickly wandered to AJ and wondered if she had called, only to get Clarissa's message. She knew AJ would call multiple times and expected to find several missed calls. She'd return her call, she knew that much, but what would she say? How would she explain her decision to leave AJ? AJ wouldn't understand, she would plead for Clarissa to reconsider her decision. She would try to convince Clarissa that she could protect her from De Marcus, but he was her master and she was his to claim, whether she wanted to go with him or not.

Once her phone finally lit-up, there were no waiting messages, no text messages, nothing. Her heart sunk. Where was AJ? Why hadn't she called for their dinner date? AJ wasn't one to overwork. Her time off the clock was important to her, she worked to stay busy, but she didn't need to work. Pushing speed dial, Clarissa put the phone on speaker and laid it on the coffee table. Her knee bounced waiting for AJ to pick up, but the phone went to voice mail. Clarissa froze. Something was wrong. AJ would never miss a dinner date, ever.

Chapter Nineteen

Selene rubbed her fingers. They stuck together from the coating of Francesca's blood. Emotions roiled inside, leaving her thoroughly and completely disgusted with herself. She sickened at the realization she had let her lust take over when the opportunity had presented itself. Her skin prickled as her mind relived the events that had just played out on her desk. Papers and office supplies scattered across the floor, further evidence of her carelessness. She'd thought about Francesca ever since they'd met and now she was responsible for taking her virginity. How did someone stay a virgin in this day and age? Impossible. Francesca hadn't confirmed she was a virgin, but it was obvious the minute Selene pushed her fingers into her. The resistance, the blood and the gasp were all confirmation of only the second time in Selene's life she had been with a virgin.

❧ ❧ ❧ ❧

A quick glance around and Clarissa was instantly taken back to the last time she'd been at the Dungeon. Her own bondage experience had helped to keep her from doing something she might regret later. Selene had been her salvation that night without knowing it and tonight she just might be her savior again.

"Clarissa, *mon Dieu!* It's been a while. How are

you? What can we do for you tonight?" Jax said, his warm voice caressing her ear.

"Jax, it *has* been a while hasn't it? I'm sorry friend." She took his extended hand. "I'm not here for a social visit. Is Selene around? I need to see her."

Clarissa hurried towards the back. Time was fleeting and AJ was in danger. She knew it now and she needed Selene to help her find her lover.

"She's not seeing anyone Clarissa. She's had a rough night." Jax grabbed her as she tried to rush past him.

Clarissa's fangs popped, her body convulsed as she seized Jax's hand, peeling it off her arm and twisting it back. Her first impulse was to break his wrist. He would not prevent her from doing what she came to do. Feeling his hand crumple under her grasp, she threw it back at him and sneered. "Back the fuck off, Jax. This isn't a social call."

"Fuck, I think you broke my wrist."

She wasn't feeling apologetic, so she didn't pretend to be sorry. Her only mission was to find out where AJ was and help her. Her stride matched her intent as she made her way back to Selene's office. A pale woman passed her in the hall, reeking of sex and blood. Confusion from the woman buffeted Clarissa and she hesitated briefly focusing on the platinum blonde in the dark passage. *Oh, Selene was busy was she?* Clarissa turned her fear into anger and directed it towards the woman in the office. She banged through the door, slamming it against the wall, and caught Selene off guard. Before she could say anything Selene had her pinned to the wall by her throat. The smell of more blood flooded her senses and she reacted. With a strong shove against Selene's chest that knocked her to the floor.

"What the fuck, Clarissa?"

Selene stood and launched herself again towards Clarissa. The two women clashed, each with their own agenda. They gripped each other's neck, fangs bared and ready to duel. Clarissa used Selene's moving body against her, slinging her over her hip and sending her crashing to the floor with a thud. Landing on top, she went for Selene's neck without another thought. Instinct took over and survival was her only goal, the person under her didn't matter in the eternal quest to survive. Clarissa felt the urge to feed, guttural in its nature. She embraced it. Inhaling she scent of saliva and blood, mixed with sex and something else—aggression—permeated the air. A vampire's worst vices, all in one hot, small space.

"STOP!" Selene commanded. Her nails dug deeper, sinking closer to the bone.

Clarissa's fangs pierced her skin, and her tongue slid against the wet trail of blood running down Selene's neck. Before she could take another swipe with her tongue, Selene heaved her off and threw Clarissa back onto the couch. Clarissa raked her nails against Selene's arms, trails of destruction evidence of her rage.

"STOP, Clarissa. What the fuck is wrong with you?" Selene pinned her against the couch with a knee in her ribs and fingers driving into her hair, jerking her head back. "If you don't stop, I'll kill you." Their gazes locked, each woman competing for dominance.

Clarissa tried to take a deep breath, her body burning with each inhale. "Off."

"Are you done?"

"OFF, Selene. I can't breathe."

Selene hesitated then lifted herself off Clarissa. Standing before her, the square set of Selene's jaw bunched each time she clenched. Clarissa felt her blood vibrate through her body. She couldn't answer for her behavior, the aggression wasn't something she couldn't relate to. It had been decades since she'd felt so helpless and lashed out.

"What the fuck is wrong with you, Clarissa?" Selene ran her palm across her neck, fingering the still oozing puncture wounds.

Clarissa fought against a wave of dizziness. She cradled her face in her palms and tried to control her breathing. It was hot in the tight confines of the office. Tossing the drapes back, she flung open the window and swayed against the sash, bracing herself on the frame. The coolness of the night felt good. The darkness felt better. Staring out past the cars, her ears perked when she heard something groaning.

"Is someone in the basement?" Clarissa said into the darkness.

"Answer my question — what the hell is wrong with you?"

Leaning against the sill, Clarissa stared at Selene. She noticed Selene's jaw bunching as she clamped it shut. How could she lose control like that? She was a pacifist, unheard of in the vampire ranks, but she'd had enough violence to last a lifetime. That was until tonight.

"I don't know. I mean…I came here to ask for help, but…that girl who just left…who is she? You're girlfriend?"

Selene threw herself into the desk chair and slouched down. Her long lanky frame stretched out reminded Clarissa of a gazelle, quick, lean and ready to run.

"It's complicated."

"It always is, isn't it?"

"Why did you come here? Shouldn't you be home with AJ having meatloaf or something?" Selene sneered at the domesticity of their situation.

"AJ didn't come over tonight and she isn't home. I think something's happened."

"What makes you think something happened?"

"I felt it in a dream."

"A dream."

"Don't make fun of me Selene. You know vampires form a connection to their mates. We can communicate without saying a thing. She knows me better than I know myself. She wouldn't go an hour without calling me, or sending me a text, communicate with me in some way." Clarissa sniffed the air. Another vampire was close by.

"So, maybe she got caught up at work." Selene cleaned a nail, trying to act as uninterested as possible. It was all a bluff and Clarissa knew it, AJ was Selene's only friend in this world all the others long dead by now.

"Who's in the basement?" Clarissa asked, knowing Selene could handle the verbal whiplash with such a sudden subject change. "I can smell them from up here." She spread her hand out as if doing so would bring them forward.

"It's that asshole from your job. I stuck him in the basement until I can figure out what to do with him."

"You kidnapped him? Oh shit." Clarissa ran her fingers through her hair. What had Selene done? They could go to jail for kidnapping. Hell they'd kill them for just being vampires, kidnapping was only an excuse. Times were changing and every vampire needed to stay two steps to the right side of the law.

"Relax, he's a vampire, too." Selene nursed the bloody streaks along her arm. Flinching as she applied a wet rag, wiping the drips of blood from her arms. "God, Clarissa. What's come over you? You're not usually the violent one in the relationship."

"I had a dream. AJ's in danger. She never came over for dinner or called."

"Came over?"

"It's a long story— well not really, but I've moved back to my place." Clarissa took the rag from Selene and dabbed at the scratches. She'd dug deep, leaving long furrows. They'd heal, but it didn't stop Clarissa from feeling stupid. She'd let her emotions control her actions. Stupid. Her mind was racing with thoughts of AJ being in danger and her aggression levels were off the chart. Selene confirming Carol's substitute was a vampire only added to her agitation.

"What was your dream about?" Selene grasped Clarissa's chin and lifted her face to see her eyes. "What about AJ?"

Clarissa was sure Selene had experienced her own dream state that gave her warning about an impending danger. She understood the affects dreams had on a person's mental state. You were always waiting for the other shoe to fall. Dreams were rarely wrong.

"She's in danger, Selene. I need your help to find her."

"Did you call her at home? I'm sure she's sitting at the penthouse waiting for you to call her. Why don't you give her a ring?" Selene pulled her arms back from Clarissa's ministrations so she could call.

"I already tried, she doesn't answer. See for yourself." Clarissa passed the ringing phone to Selene.

They waited, each woman hoping for the same outcome. Staring down at the phone, AJ's picture taking up the whole screen, she watched the moving phone as it rang, and rang again, then to voice mail. Stopping the call, Clarissa stuffed it into her pocket and sat back on the couch, burying her head in her hands.

"I'm scared, Selene."

Nothing.

"Didn't you hear me? I had a dream and she's in danger. I'm scared."

"I'll make a few phone calls and see what I can find out."

"Do you know where she is?" Clarissa stared at Selene with eyes red from crying. Her mind went somewhere she didn't want to follow and right now she felt Selene was her only hope in finding AJ.

"Is there something you're not telling me Selene?"

Chapter Twenty

Francesca ran to her car and threw the remnants of her torn clothing inside. She leaned against the door and bent over trying to catch her breath. She hurt in a way she never expected it would when she'd imagined having sex for the first time. Her body shivered through the remnants if an orgasm. If she were honest with herself, she'd give anything to be wrapped around Selene right now, experiencing a repeat performance with those skilled hands.

The distant hum of her cell phone ringing caught her attention. She peered into the car. Somewhere in that mess of clothing, paper and books was her purse and her lifeline buried inside. Leaning in, she shuffled through the mess, but the phone stopped before she could find it. Undeterred she tossed a few items on the floorboard and finally found her small clutch. Why couldn't she carry one of those big, reflective, gaudy gold-chained purses like all her friends did? They stuck out like sore thumbs and no missed them, even in a blizzard. That's why she didn't carry one, she didn't need the "look at my overpriced piece of crap that I paid way too much for" attention. If it wasn't for butt-packs being out of style she'd be wearing one right now and she would have her phone in her hands and not looking at another missed call.

Success. Her purse had landed between the door

and the seat and it was ringing off the hook again. Without looking at the number she slid it open and answered.

"Yeah."

"Yeah, you're gone for hours and all you got is yeah?" The voice on the other end scolded.

"Daph, sorry. I was busy and I couldn't get to the phone when you called."

"Whadda ya mean, when I called?"

"You didn't call me a second ago?"

"Nope, wasn't me. But that doesn't answer my question, where have you been? I've been worried sick. It's late, there weren't any lights on in the apartment, and you've been gone for hours. Where are you?"

"I…I…uhm, I worked late at the lab tonight. You know what a slave driver my boss is, phew. I'm glad today's over," Francesca lied, it killed her but she needed time to think about what happened tonight, digest everything and analyze it before she was given the third degree by Daphne. Once she'd told her roommate where she had been the grilling would start and she wasn't ready, not yet.

"So are you coming home then?"

"On my way."

"Good, can you pick-up Chinese on the way home?"

"Sure, the usual?"

"Sounds good to me, don't forget the hot mustard and fortune cookies."

"I wouldn't think of it."

"Good and be ready to talk about what really happened tonight," Daphne said before ending the call.

"Shit."

Francesca leaned against the headrest. Why

did she have to hesitate with her answer? Daphne knew her better than anyone else. Her moods, her mannerisms and she knew Francesca stuttered when she was nervous.

"Problems?"

Francesca practically jumped out of her skin when the someone pulled the door handle, so engrossed in her replay of her phone conversation, she didn't hear anyone walk up to her open car door. She should have closed it, but once again, her mind wasn't where it should have been.

"No, no it's fine thanks." She tried to shut the car door but met resistance. *Oh god, please don't let this be happening.*

"I'm not going to hurt you. I just saw you sitting here while I walked my friend to her car. I thought I better check in and make sure you're all right."

Realization sunk in with the familiar voice. Selene. *Fuck, fuck, fuck.* Of all people she *didn't* want to see. Shielding her eyes from the streetlight, she could barely make out Selene's features. The woman who had passed her in the hallway parked a few cars over and was now leaving. Shit.

"I'm good, thanks." Tucking her other leg into the car, Francesca wished to be anywhere but here with Selene.

Silence.

"I'm sorry about what happened back in there. I mean, you did all the right things and I took advantage of the power dynamic. That should never have happened. I hope you'll accept my apology."

"Nothing ttto apologize for...for...really. It's all good, I...I...I'm...ffffine. Really." Shit, she was stuttering again. She could keep it under control her whole life, but for some reason being around Selene made her lose all restraint. Closing her eyes she took a deep breath, let it out slowly and opened them to find Selene kneeling down getting ready to touch her. Jerking away, Francesca cringed at her reaction when she saw Selene's face. She doubted the woman ever showed any emotion, but the pained, apologetic expression practically sunk Francesca's heart.

"Sorry. I'm just a little…I mean…I'm…oh fuck I don't know what I mean." Francesca offered a pathetic half smile and looked away. Shame was surely written all over her face. She was ashamed for liking what had happened back in the club, ashamed for wanted a replay of the events. But most of all the shame that all Selene would have to do was invite her back in and she was certain she would follow like a puppy dog happily wagging its tail behind her owner. Did she just refer to Selene as her owner? Oh she was in worse shape than she thought. She shook her head.

"Would you like to come back in–"

"No, no I need to go pick up Chinese food for my roommate. She's waiting at home for me, and I need to go, now." Francesca mumbled as she fumbled for her keys.

"Oh, a roommate, I didn't know." Selene stood and reached for the car door.

Francesca could hear something in her voice that made her alarms go off. She'd misunderstood the roommate comment.

"Oh, she's not a *roommate*, roommate. Daphne is just a roommate. I mean, we've been roommates since college and she has a boyfriend, but she's not ready to get married or anything and well I don't have anyone or anything, I just…" She was rambling again. Hitting her head against the steering wheel she paused, wishing this night would finally end. Or, at least the forces at work could make sure she would die from painful embarrassment, thus ending her torment in front of this beautiful woman.

"I understand, I think. Well, I tried to call you to apologize, so if you check you're messages and don't recognize the number that would be me."

"Oh, that was you earlier. I thought it was Daphne. Sorry. I mean you're nothing like her or anything like that, but I just thought that it was her, since she's the only person whoever calls me." Francesca slapped her hands over her mouth to stop the info dump she was spewing all over Selene. God, she was an idiot. Would this night never end?

"Well, I should let you go. If you…well I mean…I left you a message. Let me know if you need anything."

"Can I ask you a question?"

"Sure."

"Just curious, how did you get my number?"

"Your application." Selene looked down at her, then gave her a lopsided grin. "Well you better get going, Daphne wants Chinese food."

"Oh right, yeah, I…" Francesca pointed to her phone. "Yeah, I better get going. She gets cranky when she hasn't eaten."

"I know the feeling," Selene said in a low sultry tone that made Francesca's toes curl. "I know the feeling."

Chapter Twenty-one

AJ slipped in and out of consciousness. She struggled to focus on the shaft of light that slid under the door into her dark cell.

AJ, get up, baby.

"I can't, Clarissa. I want to, but I can't." AJ could barely whisper her answer.

Baby, you need to do something.

"What?"

Your pocket. Remember the pills Doctor Swartz gave you?

Her body was so dehydrated that she couldn't produce tears as she started to cry. The tin container had spilled out all over the floor, rubbing salt into the wound of her death. Her hand slid across her pants and abs, searching for just one of the pills that could mean the difference between life and death. If she could push herself back on to the floor, maybe she would find at least one. Trying to push to one side, she grabbed at the edge of the bench, trying to pull herself over. Her muscles shook with strain the harder she pulled on the bench. She held on desperately, sliding along the edge, until her grip gave out and she collapsed onto her back.

Get the fuck up, AJ Fight! Fight for us damnit.

AJ clenched her jaw. Her throat was almost closed tight, signaling how close she was to dying. She relaxed her body and with one final heave, she tossed herself on the floor. Hitting so hard she blacked out for a moment, the pain sliced across her skull from the point of impact to her forehead. Hematoma might be a problem if she had any blood in her body. Lucky for her she wasn't going anywhere soon. The cold cement floor only added to her deathly discomfort. Searching the floor closest to her, she spotted something. Could it be one of her tablets? Stretching forward in desperation, she tried to reach the tiny red capsule. Her fingertips barely touched it enough to push it further away. Fuck.

She gasped for breath, the strain on her body evident as sweat coated her skin, cold and clammy. The beat of her heart barely registered, her breathing became labored, each effort strained beyond its limits. Staring straight ahead she lost focus, the sliver of light that seeped under the door was starting to dim. Her mind wandered to what it would be like to die. Would it hurt? She's killed so many that taking a life without thought never crossed her mind. What did they think about when she drained them of life? Did they lie there wondering, why them? Perhaps, they thought of moments they lost, loves they'd miss, or the life they'd had. Her life wasn't flashing before her eyes. In fact, she could scarcely keep a coherent thought, outside of trying to stay alive. She'd heard of people floating above themselves when they were in the throes of death and yet, here she sat on the cold, wet floor of a cell. No floating. Clarissa, she would miss Clarissa. What would Clarissa do without her? De Marcus had made it clear he would take her back, exert his master position over her. Everything she enjoyed would be taken from her and she would be his slave again. Her life would...her life...would end.

Turning her head to the other side she studied the floor. The darkness under the bed showed nothing. She was without hope, without strength and would die alone, with no one to comfort her in her final hours. She needed Clarissa to know she was her last thought before she died. She punctured her finger with her razor sharp fang and squeezed the tip, a few drops of precious blood seeped out. What energy she had, she turned to her side and started to scrawl out, AJ loves Clarissa. Surrounding it with a heart was juvenile but she feared she didn't have enough time for a letter. Pausing to catch her breath, she rested her head on her arm. She couldn't see her artwork under the bed, but it would stay protected there, safe from prying eyes. Squeezing her finger again, the drops smaller now, she pushed her finger up making the side of the heart that would encapsulate her final thoughts. She felt something. Squinting in the darkness she tried to see what it was, but could only feel a slight tap as she pushed further. Probably a rat turd, she thought, all energy depleted. Death was moments away, she was sure. Lacking any more strength, her hand flopped to the floor and the foreign object under her palm popped. Rat shit didn't pop, squish maybe, rock solid maybe, but not pop.

Isabella writing as Jett Abbott

Chapter Twenty-two

Francesca balanced the Chinese food against her hip as she tried to slip her key into the lock. The door swung wide, and Daphne stood with her hand on her hips, smiling.

"Finally. I'm starving," she said, grabbing the box of delectable food. "What took you so long? I thought maybe I would have to send a search party for you."

Daphne popped open each box of food, the steam escaping and filling the room with tantalizing aromas. Sliding a pair of cheap chopsticks out of their sleeve, she grabbed a carton and headed for the couch.

"So, where were you all night? And…don't give me that crap about work." Daphne said around a mouth full of broccoli beef.

"Didn't you mother tell you it isn't polite to talk with your mouth full?" Francesca schooled. She darted for the bathroom and a much needed shower. Hot water would exorcise her demons. It always did wonders to clear her head after her mental gymnastics from work and she suspected it would be her sanctuary now as well.

Gently she peeled her slacks down. The red welts from the flogger were a soft pink now and didn't smart as much as they had when she put her pants on. Her blouse, now that would be a different story. It stuck to her the moment she put it on and the patterned fabric hid the small trails of blood that dotted her back. Stepping into the shower with it on she let the hot water loosen the bloody contacts. Slipping it off her shoulder and to the floor, she hesitated to turn her back to the full spray of the hot shower. She knew the physics of the pressure from the pulsing hot water making contact with bruised skin would leave a less than desirable result.

"What the fuck happened to you?"

Francesca turned to hide her back and in the process jerked in pain as the water stream made contact with the lash marks.

"Don't you ever knock? I'm starting to think your mother didn't teach you anything about manners did she, Daphne?" Pulling the curtain closed, she staggered against the cold tile of the shower. *Too much cold*, she jerked off the tiles. *Fuck.*

"Who did that to you, Francesca? I'm calling the police." Daphne's voice faded as she marched into the living room, probably searching for her cell phone.

Francesca grabbed a towel and ran after Daphne. She couldn't let Daphne do anything that would hurt Selene, especially when she'd asked to be hurt.

"You are not calling the police. Give me that." Francesca reached for the phone.

"What do you mean I'm not calling the police? Someone hurt you and you need medical attention. Look at your back and legs Francesca." Daphne tried to get a peek around Francesca's toweled body. "Who did that to you?"

"Sit." Francesca pointed to the couch. "Now." Her tone left few options but to be followed.

Daphne sat down, suddenly finding her broccoli beef more interesting as she poked around in the container. A blush covered her face and Francesca knew realization had suddenly set in. She'd been to the Dungeon.

"I need a shower, can I trust you to sit still while I shower and then I can tell you all about it." Francesca tapped her on her head, making Daphne look up.

"Yes," Daphne acquiesced, looking more like a child who'd been caught with her hand in the cookie jar than a grown woman. "Promise you'll tell me everything?" she asked, suddenly perking up.

"Maybe."

"Well." Daphne shooed her with her chopsticks. "Hurry, I want to hear all about it."

"Promise me you won't call anyone, Daphne. No one."

She held up three fingers, then crossed her heart and promised.

Francesca wished she could feel relieved, but knowing that she had to share the experience with Daphne gave her little time to think about what had happened between her and Selene. She wasn't good at lying, it wasn't something she had practice with, and to be a good liar you had to do it regularly. What exactly had happened between her and Selene? A dominate/submissive relationship in the beginning, but then something else had taken over when she went to Selene's office. The ache between her legs was proof of that experience.

The shower was quick, efficient and hot. Wrapping herself in her fluffy robe, she slipped her feet into her fuzzy pink slippers and wiggled her toes in their softness. A quick glance at her image in the mirror and she was about as ready as she could be to relay the events of the evening.

"Any food left?"

"Of course, I put together a plate for you. It's in the microwave."

Daphne had made her own quick change and was the epitome of comfort, yet stylish. Her designer yoga pants, topped with a silky camisole, and hotel quality robe made Francesca feel like Daphne was slumming, sitting with Francesca. The only thing missing was a pair of red-soled designer slippers. They made 'em, Daphne just didn't want to get them dirty walking around their apartment.

"Thanks." Francesca pulled the hot plate from the microwave. She found a fork and was ready to do damage to the steaming meal. Before she could sit down, Daphne stood and made room for her on the couch.

"Sit, wait...but before you do...show me." Daphne nodded at Francesca's back.

"I need to eat first." Gingerly, Francesca sat on the sofa, shifting to find a comfortable spot on her body. Daphne didn't say anything, she just watched Francesca with a smile that could only be described as *Cheshire* at best. The silence that passed between them was weird for someone like Daphne, who was used to talking the peel off a banana.

"So, let me guess. You went to the Dungeon. You sly fox, you. I didn't think you had it in you. What was it like? Was it as exciting as watching? Who put those marks on you? What did he look like? Was he–"

"Stop." Francesca put her food on the coffee table and cupped her hands around the hot tea. Closing her eyes, she breathed deeply and sighed. This was going to be tougher than she thought. It was like sharing your most intimate thoughts, but you didn't want too. Francesca hadn't even had time to process what happened earlier and now all she wanted to do was crawl into bed and sleep. She was so tired, she could barely keep her eyes open. Her emotions had gone from one extreme to another, sexually heightened to shame and doubt. "I'm too tired for this, Daphne. Can we do this in the morning? Please?"

Daphne slid over and wrapped her arms around Francesca and suddenly she was crying. She didn't know why, but it felt good, a release of all the pent up energy she had experienced came out in a rush of emotion.

"It'll be okay," Daphne said, gently rocking Francesca back and forth.

"It's not that, really. It's just…I don't know…it's just been a roller coast of a day." Wiping at her eyes she stood and brushed her robe. "I think I just need to go to bed, Daph. Can we please talk about this in the morning?"

"Sure sweetie, but you have to promise you'll tell me all the gory details. Promise?"

"Thanks." Francesca grabbed her cell phone off the table and shut her bedroom door, leaning her head against it. Her mind was a mash-up of images, all rolling through like a silent movie. Looking at her cell phone she noticed someone had called before Daphne and left a message. She didn't recognize the number, so she scrolled through the list of missed calls. She remembered Selene had told her earlier that she'd left her a message. That was the only time the number came in. Sitting on the bed, she hit voice mail and waited. She had to make sure it wasn't someone from work that she just didn't recognize their number.

The low, sultry voice made her feel weak, and

brought a flush of heat to her face as she recognized Selene's voice. "Francesca, this is Selene. I...um, well I just wanted to-"

Francesca snapped the phone shut. She didn't want to hear how sorry Selene was for what happened tonight. She wasn't sorry. She'd signed up for the session knowing what she was getting herself into. Anything beyond that was between two consenting adults. The vision of Selene's head between her legs made her tingle. Closing her eyes and leaning back, she slid her hand between the folds of her robe, touching herself. The slick, wet lips parted for her just like they had when Selene had stroked her with her tongue. She jerked as her finger flicked across her clit. Her body wasn't alien to her, but it was rare that she explored it for pleasure. Spreading the robe wider, Francesca let her hands roam over her body, following the curves and contours. Her lips hardened with barely a touch and her mind remembered Selene's warm tongue laving over the peaks that pebbled and tightened. Francesca couldn't help herself, she hit her voice mail again and waited for the low rumble of Selene's voice to come on.

"Francesca, this is Selene. I...um, well I just wanted to talk to you. I...it's...well what I'm trying to say is it's been a while since a woman has made me lose control like that and I wish I could say I was sorry, but to be honest, I've been thinking about you since you came in with your group. I didn't mean to be disrespectful when I asked about your being a virgin. I just wanted to make sure that I didn't hurt you. If I'd have known I probably wouldn't have...scratch that, I would have still made love to you, but maybe it would have been different." The message paused and then Selene spoke again. "Look, I have an errand to run, but I wonder if you might like to have lunch, well maybe coffee would be better. Just to talk, of course. Call me if you're interested. No sex, I promise."

The call ended with the usual instructions for deleting, saving or ending the call.

Just listening to Selene's voice had been enough to send Francesca over the edge as she worked herself into a frenzy. She felt like she was being thrown against the breaking waves as her orgasm crashed around her. Shuddering, she squeezed her legs together, bit her lip and tasted blood.

"No sex, I promise," she remembered Selene saying. "But what if I need you to touch me again, Selene?" Her name hung on her lips as she drifted into the arms of sleep.

Chapter Twenty-three

Selene waited for Ian at the coffee shop near the club. She'd changed the meeting place when a little bastard had shown up at Clarissa's office. Marshal was still tucked away nicely in her basement where he belonged, at least for now. He wasn't important enough to be a pawn, maybe a small fish in a big pond, but she knew he was connected to this whole thing in some way.

Clarissa was positioned on the other side of the barrier, where she could listen to the whole exchange with Ian. While he was a vampire too, he wouldn't be able to pickup on Clarissa as easily as if she fed on human blood. It left a scent trail a blind hound dog could follow. Selene's own recent human feeding would trigger Ian's olfactory nerves, knocking them off the charts. She still wore the same clothes she had worn earlier when she fucked Francesca, all in an effort to bring Ian to his senses, so to speak. He'd have a hard time not letting it trigger his own change. This should be interesting, she thought as she sipped her tea.

Selene?

Clarissa?

Selene, I'm having a hard time sitting here with that woman's scent all over you. Can't you change your shirt at least?

*It's all part of the plan, Clarissa. If you're having a

hard time and you don't feed on human blood, imagine the hell Ian is going to go through when he sits down. It's all part of the plan. He knows where AJ is and we need him to talk. I don't have time to play his game, so be patient and let me do what I'm good at.

I hope you're right. I can feel AJ's in danger and I don't think we have much time.

I know, I know.

"Selene, there ya are girl. How've ya been?"

Selene stood and just as she thought, Ian wrapped her in a bear hug pulling her off her feet. Giving her a peck on the cheek, he leaned back and leered at her. "You've been busy," he said, sitting her down.

She hadn't washed her face, barely wiped the wetness off, so she knew Francesca was all over where he had just placed his lips. Target located. He might tag on her scent, but he would never get close enough to Francesca for Selene to worry. Sitting down across from him, she noticed the instant glassy-eyed look on his face, he was reveling in the array of scents that she was giving off.

"Thanks for meeting me here, Ian. Sorry, I had an emergency come up here making it impossible to get to the low valley."

"No problem, girl. Next time you can come over to me gaff and we'll get a couple of gingernuts, that is if you favor the reds."

Disgusting, all Ian thought about was feeding his dick and money, and if the two went hand in hand, he was a happy camper. Part him from one of those things and he became the demon you never wanted as an enemy.

"Did you bring the money?"

Before he could answer a waitress interrupted

them. *Fuck*, she just wanted to part him from his money, get the information she needed and be on her way. Luck was never on her side.

"Calm down Selene, we'll take care of business, but in the meantime this beautiful woman needs to make a living, dontcha girl?" Ian said, wrapping his arm around her hips, pulling her closer. Poor thing never knew what hit her as she giggled and stared at his baby blues. "I'll have a dark ale. You do have those here dontcha? Selene, what'll you have? One of those prissy drinks with an umbrella?"

"I have my tea," she said rocking the mug in her hand.

"Bring her a prissy drink with one of those umbrellas and two cherries. She likes fruit in her drink, if you know what I mean." He slapped her ass as she walked away still giggling. "So Selene, I have this problem as you know. I need you to take care of it as soon as possible."

"Money?"

Patting his chest, he said, "Right here. I'll pass it to ya as soon as we work out the details."

"We worked out the details, Ian. This meeting is just a formality." She pointed back and forth between them. "You just need to tell me where De Marcus is and pass me the ball."

"Ah, here we are, a dark ale for your sir," the waitress said, placing the frosty glass in front of Ian. "And here we go for you, ma'am." Smiling, she placed a tall glass with brightly colored liquid in front of Selene.

"What is it?"

"It's called Sex with Jennifer. It's my favorite." She winked at Selene.

"Really, well thank you, Jennifer."

"Oh that's not my name, it's the name of the drink." The waitress giggled.

"I kinda figured."

"Oh, you were being funny. I'm sorry." Turning towards Ian, she asked, "Is there anything else?"

"Not yet, my sweet, but check back in about ten minutes and I'll be ordering another one of these if I like it."

Walking away the waitress giggled some more and Selene just shook her head. Ian was beyond unbelievable. No doubt he'd have the waitress bedded before the night was over.

"So Selene, where were we?"

"De Marcus. Where is he?"

Stroking his chin, Selene could hear the coarse stubble sanding his fingers as he slid them back and forth. He was stalling, but why? Either he was here on De Marcus' behalf or he really wanted De Marcus dead.

"You didn't hear this from me, get it?" His gaze shifted around the room as he leaned in and sniffed in Selene's direction. He stalled again, letting the smell of her last feeding envelop him.

"Ian."

"You smell divine, my girl. Male or female?"

"What?"

"The person you feed on, I can smell them on you. Young, nubile and fresh. Virgin?"

Selene sat back in her seat, trying to put some distance between them. Ian was starting to freak her out. Their business needed to conclude as soon as possible or he would be her next entree.

"I haven't heard the answer to my question, Ian.

Spill." Her voice was menacing as she reached down into her boot and fingered the stiletto nested safely.

"I heard that De Marcus was at the coven today. Something about taking care of some business there. I figured he pinched Butch, but the bastard called me today about something else, so *he's* alive and well."

"So where's De Marcus? Is he still there?"

"Naw, he finished his work there and now he's here, searching for some property that belongs to him."

"Property?" *Clarissa*.

"Yeah, I don't know what that means. The bastard has his fingers in a lot of crap, that's why I want him gone. Some of that is my crap, and I ain't sharin', if you know what I mean."

"Yeah, I'm reading you all right."

"Good, now when will you have the job done?"

"I need a little more information than, *he's here*. Who's at the coven?"

Ian shrugged, watching women at another table rehashing their night at the club.

"Ian." Selene snapped her fingers.

"What?"

"Who was at the coven today?"

"According to someone I know, it's an outlier. She's a pain in Butch's ass and he wanted to end that pain, if you know what I mean."

"Yeah, I know what you mean." Selene knew exactly who Ian was talking about. AJ was at the coven. She checked her watch. If she was right, AJ had been there for more than a couple of hours. Nothing good would come from her being there, nothing.

Ian slid a brown paper bag across the table in front of her. "Here's the first half of the payment as agreed. You'll get the rest when I get De Marcus' head."

"On a pike or have we graduated to a box? Selene said, thumbing through the hundreds, just as she'd ordered.

"A picture will do just fine, lass."

Stuffing the money back in the bag, she pushed it in her back pocket and slid across the seat closer to Ian. "If you try and fuck me over, I'll find you, cut your head off and stick it on the biggest pike I can find and put it on the busiest road for all to see. Got it?"

"You don't 'ave to be so dramatic, Selene. I've known ya now what…almost a century? In all that time have I tried to take advantage of you?" Ian smiled. "You know what I mean."

"Where is De Marcus?"

"I heard he's staying down in the seedy part of town. Doin' some recruiting of some sort."

"Great, this just keeps getting better and better, doesn't it?"

"I'm afraid not. He's got some pisser with him."

"Who?"

"Don't know, just know he's a fresh face kid."

"Gotta name to go with the description?"

"Mark, Marty–"

"Marshall?"

"Maybe." Ian grabbed his crotch and whistled. "I gotta take a leak. Be right back."

Signaling the waitress over, Selene waited until the bathroom door closed behind him before she knocked on the divider. "Can you let my friend know I had to leave?"

"Sure, Hon."

Selene slipped her a twenty and waited at the

corner for Clarissa. "We gotta go, I want to stash you somewhere safe and get to the coven."

"AJ's there, isn't she?"

Selene didn't have the heart to confirm Clarissa's worst suspicions, but odds weren't in AJ's favor right now.

Chapter Twenty-four

AJ fingered the small capsule, still not believing her luck. It stuck to her damp fingertip as she brought it to her nose for further inspection. She wasn't about to stick it in her mouth, not if it was rat shit. A shallow sniff was all she could muster, but the aroma couldn't be denied. Blood.

Crushing it further she stuffed it under her tongue, the sublingual delivery system was the fastest way to get a medication in to the blood supply if you didn't have a direct line into a vein. She closed her eyes and let the concentrated blood linger in her mouth, mixing with what little saliva she had left. She'd need another capsule or two before she would have enough strength to save her own life, let alone Clarissa's. Patience wasn't her strong suit, and waiting for the blood to do its work was exceedingly slow.

She drifted in and out of consciousness, each time her mind more lucid. Suddenly, she remembered her dinner date with Clarissa. She'd be pissed AJ had missed another one of her famous dinners. She'd think of a way to make it up to her, she always did, but she had some unfinished business with the coven's leader, Gaylord Van der Plume. She hoped Butch had enjoyed watching her almost die, because it would be her turn now.

Voices trailed down the hall, passing her door. She wanted to yell out, but thought better of it as she weighed her options. Eventually they would come and check on her, so she had to play her cards right. Rolling to her back she swept out her hands to her sides and searched for more capsules. If she found one she'd find the rest, even if it killed her. Her search wasn't in vain, as her hand rolled over another and then another. Hell, she'd be happy to find just one more, but two would give her more than hope of surviving, it would guarantee she'd live.

She needed to find the tin that held the capsules, if her captors found it they would give it to Butch and he would know she lied about having the blood substitute. So she continued to slide around on the floor searching for it. The sound of metal sliding across the floor let her know she'd found the tin box that held her capsules. Slipping one of the two capsules into the tin and back into her pocket. She crushed the second capsule and placed it under her tongue.

Her eyes slammed shut as a key rattled in the lock. The door was pushed open and light spilled into the room. Boots echoed on the stone floor. Two men, maybe more, walked towards AJ. Her eyes, barely slits, followed their movement.

"She dead yet?" A husky voiced asked.

A swift kick to her ribs forced out a short breath loud enough for the goons to hear.

"Not yet. De Marcus said it could take a couple of days, depending on the last time she fed."

"Yeah, well let's not risk it." The sound of a gun being cocked shook her, but she could barely move.

"Hey, he wants her to suffer."

"Yeah, well maybe I want to put her out of her misery. Besides, De Marcus isn't here, is he?"

"Nope, but Butch is and he's psycho lately or

haven't you noticed?"

"Yeah, I noticed. Fucking crazy-ass bastard, gives me the willies."

"Well, I don't feel like ending up like this chick here. So leave her be. Besides, I heard De Marcus talking to someone, telling 'em he was going to be taking over the coven soon."

"What do you think he means by that?"

AJ wasn't surprised at De Marcus's plans to take over the coven. She wondered if Butch knew how ruthless he could be. *Poor bastard, deserves everything he gets.*

"How much longer do you think she can last?"

She felt fingers on her neck trying to measure her pulse.

"Not much longer, she's almost dead now."

"We better let Butch know."

The solid door closed but she didn't hear it lock. *Stupid bastards.* AJ rolled to her side. Butch would want to be here when she died, in fact she was counting on it. Another hour was all she needed for the second pill to take effect.

❧❧❧❧

Clarissa needed to get to the coven. AJ was there, she knew it, she felt it, hell she *dreamed* it. Her mind raced, De Marcus was close, his minion Marshall had tipped his hand when he made such a show of introducing himself.

Carol.

Where was Carol? What had the bastard done with her? She pulled out her phone and dialed Carol's number. Carol narrowly escaped being De Marcus's victim last year at the masquerade ball. If Selene hadn't stepped in, god only knows what would have happened. She owed her an explanation, but it had never materialized. Instead, a death in Carol's family had sidelined any discussion they would have had about Carol's *creepy* ex-boyfriend. If Carol only knew how close to death she'd come that night. How could she have forgotten her closest friend?

"Hello?"

"Carol?"

"Clarissa, oh my god, I forgot to call you. I am so sorry."

Clarissa's body flooded with relief. "I was worried about you. What happened? Some guy shows up, tells me he's taking your place for the rest of the term and boom, you're gone."

"I apologize, sweetie. My brother's had a stroke, and his wife isn't in any condition to take care of him so I caught the first flight to Milwaukee. I should have called, I am so sorry."

"I'm sorry to hear about your brother. This jerk said you had a death in the family and I was worried."

'Oh, they found a replacement already? Jeez, I thought I was a little harder to replace, guess not." Carol sounded disappointed at the news of her replacement.

Selene tapped Clarissa on the arm and shook her head. Clearly, she didn't want Clarissa saying too much about *Marshall.*

"You're irreplaceable, so don't even think about not coming back." Clarissa tied to sound reassuring.

"Thanks, sweetie. It's probably going to be a few months before I can come back. My brother's pretty bad off. I need to handle his affairs and then I can come back with some peace."

"Oh, Carol, I wish I was there to help you. Is there anything I can do to help?"

"Thanks, but my other brothers are coming, so I'll have help. You can do one thing."

"Sure, anything."

"Tell my replacement not to get comfortable, 'cause he isn't staying."

"Oh, I don't think you have to worry about that," Clarissa said, watching Selene as she motioned for her to wind things up. "How about I call you in a few day and give you a progress report?"

"Sounds good. Talk to you soon."

"Bye."

She wished relief came in a bottle. She would swill it in her mouth, bath in and buy it buy the case. She was a worrier and she came by it honestly. A trait passed down from her grandmother, to her mother and now to her.

"What the hell made you do that?"

"What?"

"Call Carol." Selene tossed Clarissa a disapproving glance before she turned her attention back to driving.

"Carol's my friend. I was worried about her."

"We don't have friends, Clarissa. It never ends well for us."

"Really, so who was that cute little blond that I saw leaving your office tonight?"

"No one special," Selene deadpanned.

"So what you were thinking when I arrived doesn't–"

"I can't afford to get involved with someone, Clare. The business I'm in doesn't exactly make for good bedfellows. So she's *nobody*."

"You might be able to fool yourself, but I know what I felt, and she isn't a *nobody*, Selene."

"It doesn't matter. It's over before it started," Selene lied and Clarissa could sense the turmoil Selene was battling. She felt sorry for her old friend. She wished everyone could be as happy as she and AJ were before all of this started up again. If she was being honest with herself though, she knew she was going cut AJ off, the way Selene was doing with the cute blonde from the club. It was the only way to protect AJ from De Marcus. Clarissa was his property. He was back to claim her and she knew it.

"We're going to back to the club. I know you'll be safe there and I need to make some phone calls and see what I can find out about AJ"

"What about De Marcus?"

"Our boy Marshall will lead us to De Marcus."

"You really think he's working for him?"

"Yep." Selene pulled into her reserved parking space at the club. Turning towards Clarissa, she touched her and waited.

"What? What's wrong?" Clarissa started to panic. Selene's usually calm mind was frantic and a jumbled mess. Steeling herself, she laid her hand on top of Selene's and gave a half-hearted smile. "AJ's alive. I know it. So don't give me the 'you should prepare yourself' crap."

"Clare—"

"Don't, Selene. I'm warning you."

Chapter Twenty-five

The fucking bitch should be dead or damn close to it."

AJ heard Butch before he was halfway down the corridor. His arrogant attitude would be his downfall. She just had to be patient. Her tongue licked across dry lips. Her necked popped as she twisted it to the left and then to the right. She'd considered pushing herself up off the cold floor, but she couldn't risk exposing her advantage if the same two guards from earlier came in again with Butch.

"Open the door and let me see the bitch." Butch almost sounded gleeful as he barked out orders.

AJ lay rigid, her eyes open just enough to see the boots of the guard step closer. Only one set of boots and a pair of velvet loafers stood next to her. *Bonus.* Butch had made a tragic mistake, one she would take advantage of.

"Turn her over, I want to see her face."

A boot on her hip tried to push her over, but she held firm in her position on the floor. Unable to move her, the guard cursed and knelt down. He shoved her with his hand. AJ lunged, seizing his elbow with one hand and crotch with the other. He yelled out as she squeezed his balls. Using his body weight against him, she flipped him over her and onto the floor. He landed with a thud that drove the air out of his lungs and loosened his grip on the weapon. AJ rolled on top and snatched the rifle from his hands. With one swift thrust, she smashed the butt of the rifle into his face, and then rotated the weapon, pointing the business end at Butch. He stood rooted to the spot with his mouth agape.

"No, no, no–" he started to say, raising his hands as if they would stop a bullet.

"Shut the fuck up, Butch." AJ, still wobbly, sat on the man and tried to catch her breath. "Sit down." She pointed to the steel bed.

"You won't escape out of the coven, AJ. You know that, right?" he said, sitting gingerly on the edge of the cold metal.

"Scoot back, all the way against the wall." she ordered. Her pulse raced. A good sign the capsules were doing their job, but she needed more quickly. Pulling the guard's wrist up to her lips, her fangs popped and dropped into his vein. Her gaze stayed focused on Butch as he grimaced. "What, you get all squeamish watching others feed? That's totally out of character for you, Butch."

Blood drops splattered on the guard's shirt as she talked. She couldn't feed fast enough, but she couldn't pass up the urge to gloat, either. Pulling his wrist up further, she bit down hearing the crunch of bones breaking and tendons snapping, her reward for her feeding brutality. She had to pace herself, the loss of her own blood and the sudden replacement could make her sick. As it oozed down her throat she couldn't help but enjoy it. She was sure she would have the typical blood hangover later, from consuming it too quickly. Her body craved the replenishing, her mind demanded to be fed and her heart, well the revenge would satisfy her heart. Out of the corner of her eye she caught Butch edging down the bed towards the still open door. In a blink of an eye she was sitting next to Butch, the barrel of the gun resting against his rib cage.

"Where do you think you're going, Gaylord?" His visceral reaction to his name made her laugh. "You've been a bad boy, a very bad boy, and I plan to punish you." Her maniacal laughter echoed throughout the cell.

"If you kill me you won't get De Marcus. He's the one you want, not me."

"Okay, so tell me where De Marcus is and I'll consider sparing you."

"You will?"

"Of course, my beef isn't with you, it's with him." AJ smiled and placed her chin on his shoulder, repositioning the barrel higher up on his ribs. He flinched as she pushed the barrel against them. She wanted to hit his heart if she shot him, so she angled the rifle butt down more.

"But…I almost had you killed…I mean—" Butch shifted away from the gun.

"A minor faux pas. Now where is De Marcus?"

"I'm afraid you might be too late, Alexandra."

His use of her given name was like finger nails on a chalk board. Only Clarissa called her by her birth name. It was music on Clarissa's lips when she used it while they were in the throes of passion, but to hear it come from his lips made her sick. Holding her temper, she prodded again.

"De Marcus."

"He isn't here, he's…he's gone…to get Clarissa."

"When did he leave?"

"An hour ago. He didn't care to see your dead

body, so he left to get her."

"Give me your phone."

"What?"

"Give me your…" she pushed the barrel harder against his ribs. "cell phone. I'm sure you're like everyone else and sleep with the damn thing, so give it to me."

Nervously, he patted the chest of his velvet robe that matched his loafers and then started to run his hands down his front.

"Uh, uh, uh. Stop right there, Gaylord. Stand up and put your hands on the wall," she commanded, hoping she could do the same.

She stood, swayed towards Butch and buried the tip of the barrel into his back. Luckily he freaked and patted the wall with his hands, trying to show her he was complying with her order.

"Good, now play nice and you'll live to see another moon rise."

She reached around and patted his front found his cell phone in his pants pocket, hoping that was all she felt. After a moment of revulsion, she forced herself to reach in and extract his cell phone. She had to warn Clarissa that De Marcus was on his way.

"Drop your pants around your ankles."

"What? You can't be serious."

"I am, now do it."

She rolled her eyes at the sight of him. "Not the best day to go commando, now is it, Gaylord?"

"Can't I just put my jacket down on the floor? It's going to be cold and well my—"

"Get on the fucking floor and shut up. You're wasting precious time here, asshole."

"Fine." He flung himself on the floor, his lily-white ass mooning her.

Without a second thought, she turned the gun around and smacked him on the back of the head, crushing his skull. Shooting him would draw attention and right now she needed to be as quiet as possible to make a clean escape. Reaching over she grabbed the guard's knife, and sawed on his neck. The bastard was old and gristly. It took everything in her to finally sever his head from his body, killing him. Unsteady again, she reached for the edge of the bench behind her and sat. Slow and easy needed to be the mantra until she regained enough strength to get the hell out of the coven. Eventually, Butch would be missed and someone would come looking for him. When they did she needed to be gone.

She paused, listening for any activity outside the cell door. Nothing. She dialed the phone.

"Pickup, come on pick-up, Clarissa," she said, nervous that she'd have a visitor before she got to warn Clarissa.

"Hello, if you'd like to leave me a message, you know what to do."

Clarissa's voice sounded so good right now, if only it was really her, AJ thought. She knew if Clarissa didn't recognize the number she wouldn't answer the phone.

"Baby, it's me. I'm all right. I had some business at the coven and I'm on my way home. I should be there in about two hours. Keep dinner warm for me and make sure the alarm is set and you've locked down the elevator. I'll call you when I get to the garage and then you can unlock it. Okay? See you soon. I love you."

Fuck!

Selene.

Selene would recognize the number and take her call.

※ ※ ※ ※

Look, I'm sure AJ will call," Selene said, trying to calm Clarissa's fears. "She's just probably tied-up with work or something."

Selene slid her shades on, shielding her eyes from the light of the sunset. She wished her meeting with Ian had been somewhat productive, but she hadn't really expected much from him. She rarely agreed to meet with clients, but she wanted to look Ian in the face when she played him. He'd done exactly what Selene expected, flirt her up, give her some information and left out the most important part–how he knew so much about De Marcus. Who was he protecting?

"It's the *or something* I'm worried about."

"She's a big girl. She can take care of herself. Besides, you two are so connected to each other you'd know if something was wrong, right?" Selene knew Clarissa had every reason to worry. AJ took too many risks to get De Marcus, her anger clouded her judgment. If she wasn't careful those risks would catch up to her, eventually.

"That's exactly why I'm worried. I hear her calling out to me and I can't honestly tell you it wasn't just a dream. I just need to talk to her, that would put my mind at ease and then I'll kick her ass when I see her."

Selene's phone vibrated against her chest. Looking down at her screen, she didn't recognize the number, but the area code was the same as the one she called when she made the appointment at the coven with Butch. Hesitating, she thought about letting it go to the voicemail. She rarely picked up numbers she didn't recognize, but something about the coven calling *her* made her suspicious.

"Yeah?"

After a beat of silence, she heard a wheezing breath.

"Selene." Selene could barely recognize the haggard voice on the other end. AJ sounded like death was knocking. Another staggering breath and then she said, "If Clarissa is with you don't say my name, I don't want her to panic…"

"Okay…what's up?" Selene switched the phone to the other side hoping Clarissa couldn't recognize the voice. "I'm on my way to the club. Can I call you back at this number?"

"No, I'm…I'm on my way home, but I wanted to give you a heads up, De Marcus is on his way there."

Selene turned her head and whispered into the phone. "How do you know that? You don't sound so good."

"It's a long story, but I should be fine in a few hours. Don't send Clarissa to the penthouse. Take her somewhere safe until I get there. In fact, take her back to the club. I'll meet you there and explain everything."

"Okay, but—"

"Tell her to check her messages. I tried to call but it went to voicemail."

"Okay."

"Selene, De Marcus has associates working with him, so keep an eye out for them."

"I think I might have run into a mutual friend already."

"Shit, is Clarissa okay?"

"Just fine, thanks for asking."

"Thanks buddy, I owe you one."

"Oh, I think you owe me more than one." Selene said, trying to sound as casual as possible. "Okay travel safe and see you when you get here."

"Will do."

The line went silent before she could ask any more questions. Probably just as well considering Clarissa was sitting next to her, straining to listen.

"So who was that?"

"An old friend coming into town." Selene's answer was truthful as far as she was concerned.

"Sounds like he's sick."

"Yeah, he said he's fighting a cold."

"Ah, so he isn't one of us. Interesting, Selene. I didn't figure you for having human friends."

Vampires didn't get sick, one of the perks of being quick, self-healers. They also didn't suffer the normal living human frailties, but their burden was in how long they could live. An easier life was often small comfort for the loss and heartache endured over the centuries of a vampire's existence

"Really? Why would you think I didn't have any friends who weren't vampires?" Selene's droll tone almost confirming Clarissa's statement she was sure.

"I guess I've always thought of you as a loner. My mistake, we all change, it's inevitable. I just thought you were the one constant in all of this."

"Really?" Selene couldn't dispute the analysis, because change wasn't something she was comfortable with. She liked routine, the daily rhythm of life and for her it kept her somewhat stable, at least she liked to think it did The life of an assassin was off-kilter, nomadic at times, but her routine of tea at six every morning, training at seven and then equipment checks and maintenance forced her to try and maintain a schedule, of sorts.

"Is that all you can say?"

"Have you checked your phone lately? Maybe AJ has called."

Patting her purse, she pulled it out and showed Selene the phone face. "It's dead. My charger is in my car, so I guess I'll just–"

"Try mine, looks like we have the same phone." She pointed to the built in charger on the dash. Any distraction to get Clarissa off her back and off the subject of friends would be welcome.

"Oh, nice."

"Yeah, they do custom work at this shop. Got a few other gadgets installed for emergencies."

"Like?"

"Not important," Selene said, pulling on to the highway towards the club.

Selene was a pro at diversion and if she could take Clarissa's mind off AJ until the phone charged she'd work it. Lucky for her Clarissa had just taken the bait.

"So who was on the phone?"

Well, maybe not.

⁂

An arm over her eyes shielded her from the bright sunlight peeking through the thin drapes. Her body rebelled against the thought of getting up, but her bladder demanded action. Swinging her legs off the bed the sweet sting of pain laced her back.

"Hey, you up in there?" A light tapping followed

the inquiry.

Fuck, Daphne.

"Yeah, give me a minute. I gotta go to the bathroom." She'd only be able to stall for so long, and then the walk of shame was inevitable.

Why shame? They were two consenting adults. They didn't do anything wrong, but for some reason she a little shame mixed with her pleasure. Her face flushed as the image of Selene buried between her legs flashed. *God, I want more.*

After washing her hands and brushing her teeth she slipped a T-shirt over her head. The friction of the fabric against the raised pink lash marks made her flinch. She pulled open the door and Daphne practically fell at her feet.

"What are you doing?"

"Listening to make sure you're all right?" Daphne cocked a lopsided grin.

"Seriously?"

"No, not serious. Can I come in for some girl time?"

"Do I have a choice?"

"No."

"I didn't think so." Francesca walked to the bed.

"Oh my god, do those hurt?" Daphne pointed to the bruises peeking out from under her T-shirt bottom.

Blushing, she slipped back under the covers, pulling them up to her chin as if they would protect her from Daphne's exploring nature.

"Those look just like in that book."

"What book?"

"You know that book with that Grey guy," Daphne said, climbing in on the other side of the bed. "You know, those bondage books all the women at work are talking about." She snuggled closer to Francesca.

"Hey can I have some real estate here? This is *my* bed." Francesca reminded Daphne.

"Oh, sorry."

"So, what was it like? I mean…I wanna go."

"You can go anytime you want."

"No, I want you to take me." Daphne snuggled closer again. "Can, I touch them?"

Daphne was never going away until she got what she wanted. *Just ask her boyfriend.* Francesca rolled onto her side and slipped her T-shirt up, exposing. A cool touch traced a line across her backside and then another and another. She felt warm breath on her back. Daphne had moved in for a closer inspection.

"I can see the outline of the crop or whatever they used. Does it hurt?"

"No, I'm good. It was….I don't know…I guess it was—"

"Hot."

Francesca smiled. Oh yeah, she's hot all right.

Chapter Twenty-six

The silence in the car left Selene to struggle with the impending darkness, gnashing its teeth at the periphery of her soul. Its frayed edges signaling the impending fall into blackness. She didn't fear it. Like life, it was an inevitability that if unanswered it couldn't be avoided. She feared the loss of control that came with the darkness more. In light she could do anything, be anyone. In the dark abyss she could only be one thing, the one thing she most dreaded, an animal.

Then there were the sacred memories secluded in the catacombs of her mind. The well-lit paths were starting to dim with each successive kill. How would she get back to those treasures of her family if she continued on this path? There was no redemption for her, only pain, and she squelched that path each time she took a life. Hence the conundrum she found herself in.

There was Francesca. Without knowing why, she would find herself drawn to Selene, like a moth pulled to a glowing light, it was instinct that would pull Francesca. Selene would burn from the bright light that emanated from such an innocent and Francesca had unwillingly found herself bound to Selene when she'd given her virginity. Selene would have—no must have acted differently had she known Francesca was a virgin. The sacrificial virgin wasn't a myth in the vampire lore. It was fact. The bond of virginal blood was rare, even in modern times, but it was a bond, a pull, Selene couldn't ignore. Their bond was forged in that blood forever. Francesca belonged to her alone. It would only be a matter of time before Francesca came to her, not knowing what possessed her to seek out Selene. Was Selene ready for that?

Selene doubted she could be what Francesca required in a mate. A lover, a protector, yes, but she doubted her own mating ability. She was no AJ or Clarissa, bonded for an eternity. Francesca had no way of knowing what she had gotten herself into when she gave herself to Selene. It would be Selene's responsibility to decide Francesca's fate. Francesca wouldn't be able to decide for herself, biology would take over her logical mind and body.

"Earth to Selene." Clarissa snapped her fingers in front of Selene's face. "Hey, did you hear what I said?"

"Yeah, yeah," Selene lied.

"Really, I think you were on the blonde planet. So, what's up between you two?"

"Nothing." Selene's terse tone sending a signal she didn't want to talk about Francesca.

"Well that's not the vibe that cute little thing gave off when she passed me in the hall," Clarissa said, rubbing at the maroon polish on her fingernails. "Her body was humming as she practically ran past me. Only one thing does that to a woman...*Selene.*" Selene saw Clarissa piercing her with a *no bullshit* look.

Selene kept her eyes on the road refusing to acknowledge Clarissa's statement. But like a dog with a bone, Clarissa continued.

"Selene." Clarissa covered Selene's hand resting

on the shifter. "You've been on this path too long and I worry you'll retract into the darkness if you stay on it much longer."

"What do you mean?"

"It takes decades for those of us who are day walkers to get here in the light. But no one knows how long it would take to lose it when we decide to embrace that finger of darkness that threads its way into our soul."

If Selene didn't know better, she would have thought Clarissa had peered into her thoughts a moment ago. Selene had perfected the ability to prevent someone from intruding on her mentally. AJ, at two hundred years her senior, was the only one old enough in Selene's circle of friends who could penetrate her mind. Clarissa, while older than Selene, had been a slave too long and a submissive had baggage to overcome before she could even get close to Selene. Clarissa could connect to AJ, their bond as lovers connected them deeper than a vampire to vampire connection.

"I'm fine, trust me." She patted Clarissa's hand reassuringly and gave her a half-hearted smile. "I can't do this much longer. After De Marcus is caught or killed, I'm done."

"I'm going to hold you to that."

Looking to change the subject and get it off her, Selene quipped. "How about we just get back to the club and wait for AJ?"

"Do you think she's there?"

"Probably." Selene lied, but didn't have the heart to tell her AJ was most likely running for her life. Her comment about being "fine in a few hours" didn't sound encouraging. If she died, Selene would kick her ass. Metaphorically of course.

"God, I can't wait to put my arms around her."

"Hmm."

※ ※ ※ ※

Francesca's hand froze on the ornate brass handle on the massive door to the Dungeon. She wanted to turn and run. Her fight or flight response multiplied inside. She'd never been one to act irrationally, which is why she couldn't seem to explain what her heart was telling her head. Her body ached for attention, to relive the experience from the night before, again.

"Hey, wait up," Daphne said, following behind. "Gosh, you're in a hurry."

"Sorry, it looks like rain."

"Really?" Daphne raised her hands as if she was trying to catch a few phantom raindrops. "I don't think so, are you okay? I know I can be pushy, so if this is a bad idea we can go home."

Francesca could hear the quiver in Daphne's voice. She was all talk and little action and Francesca had called her bluff this afternoon. The taunts and chatter were driving her crazy. When she couldn't take anymore, she threw it back in Daphne's face and mounted the challenge.

"If you want to go, fine. Let's go tonight. I want you to experience this all first-hand."

Now, Francesca wished she'd kept her own mouth shut. Lately she'd felt bullied into things, like Dorothy and the night at the Dungeon. This afternoon Daphne's taunts had been the final poke. So she poked back and here she was, her hand ready to pull the door to another peek into a different world she never thought she'd ever experience again.

"Okay." Daphne grabbed Francesca's upper arm and gripped it tight. "Let's go inside."

"Look, just one thing. Please don't embarrass me. Okay?"

"What do you mean?"

"Just try and play it cool. Don't freak out, don't shout anything inappropriate, and please, please don't touch anyone or volunteer. Okay?"

"Damn, Frankie. You must think I'm some adolescent school boy, jeeze."

"In a word, yes."

"Seriously?"

Francesca just rolled her eyes at Daphne.

"Fine. Look but don't touch and no inappropriate talking. Happy?"

"We'll see."

Ducking into the dark club, Francesca pulled Daphne through the doors and into an experience she was sure would change them both.

Chapter Twenty-seven

AJ pulled the cell door closed and grabbed the keys she had fished out of the guard's pocket. A locked door kept people out, just as easily as they kept people in and by the time anyone in the coven missed Butch, she'd be long gone. Her knees shook with each step and it was clear she still needed time to rest. Hiding in the coven wasn't an option. Without a leader or a direct successor the coven would be in instant turmoil and AJ didn't need to be around when the shit hit the fan.

AJ scanned the area, checking for cameras. The coven didn't have them installed anywhere, which meant she might make it out without being seen. Slipping down the hall she listened to every sound, down to the mouse scrambling along the wall ahead of her. Her mouth watered at the thought of its warm blood pulsing through its tiny body. She hated thinking like an animal, but would do whatever it took to get back to Clarissa. Following the squeaks, she knew the mouse would lead her to an exit or at least to a dark hiding hole. Maybe not her size, but at this point she would take anything. The silence of the coven pretty much assured her that it was daylight, but she wasn't sure for how much longer. She worried about Clarissa and the head start De Marcus had on her. One thing she knew, it was long enough for De Marcus to get back to the bay area and get to Clarissa.

A sense of relief flooded her, she was lucky Selene had taken her call, Clarissa was safe and in good hands.

Footfalls drawing closer made her scramble for cover. Slipping into a dark room, she waited just inside the door for the person to pass. She briefly contemplated pulling them into the room and draining them, but another body plus Butch's disappearance would be hard to hide without alerting someone. The sound of a heartbeat stopped her, then another and another and…all pulsing in the room. She was in a den of sleeping vampires. Her heart raced with one thought running through her mind: *Run!*

Slipping her head out the door, she watched another guard slowly make her way down the hallway. Peering towards her exit she waited until she thought the coast was clear and snuck quietly out of the room. Sweat slipped between her breasts and down her back. At least her body was starting to function. Now it was imperative to make her way to freedom and safety. Time wasn't her friend, she needed to make a quick exit and return to Clarissa.

"The others should be rousing soon, come here." A voice somewhere behind her whispered.

Great, I roll right into a sex scene, wonder if they'd be interested in a three-way? Sarcasm was the only way AJ could handle the situation as she tried to block out the sounds of flesh slapping.

A scream broke the silence, rousing vampires from their waning sleep. It was only a matter of time before the coven became active again and her cover would be blown. Reaching for the nearest door handle she opened it, hoping it didn't lead to another den of vampires. The darkness while inviting came with the fear of not knowing what was inside. Her eyesight weakened just like her body, impaired her ability to see any great depth. Pounding footsteps made her rush inside. She'd take her chances with a few over the many that would respond to the blood curdling scream. Obviously, someone had found Butch and now they would mount a full-scale effort to find his killer and the only person supposed to be in that cell: AJ.

A coat closet, she was in a damn closet. She fumbled around, searching around for something more than fabric, something she could use to protect herself. Riffling through pockets, she was coming up empty. Pushing the coats aside, she searched deeper into the bowels of the closet. The space didn't end. She moved deeper and deeper behind the jackets. Was this a passageway? Darkness enveloped her the farther she moved into the closet. Dank musty air pricked her nostrils, wetness sloshed around her feet. *I hope that isn't something other than water.* The floor sloped downward into a void. She kept moving. The unknown was better than staring down the barrel of a rifle. She just had no way of knowing where it did end up, but she'd rather take her chances in the blackness of the tunnel, as long as it led her away from the coven and to freedom.

Inching further into the darkness, all she wanted to do right now was rest. Her body ached as it tried to replenish the blood she'd lost. Her enhanced capsules were working, but she was just this side of death and escaping its clutches her body started to swell. Her muscles were finally becoming engorged with her own blood and the fog her mind mingled in was slowly starting to clear. She'd need to give Dr. Swartz a pay raise for the improved formula. Sliding down against the wall she squatted, trying to rest. AJ cradled her pounding head in her hands and slowed her breathing. She didn't want to waste valuable energy overtaxing her heart and spending what she didn't have to lose. Closing her eyes, she focused her other senses to engage her surroundings—no movement anywhere. In fact, it seemed even her mouse had deserted her, too. Her mind drifted to Clarissa, the last time they cradled each other in bed. The pillow talk moments kept them wound tighter together than anything else they could do. Often times they shared bits and pieces of their past. They could spend eternity in cuddle mode and never cover all that had happened in their lives.

Leaning her head against the damp cement wall, she dozed quietly for a few minutes. She faced a dilemma–take another concentrated capsule or find someone to feed on. Blood from someone would heal her more efficiently than waiting for the concentrate to work, but it would have lingering affects to her mentally. The mental orgasm a vampire received when they fed off a body was like playing with fire for her. She'd abstained for so long and yet in one day she had swallowed more blood than she had in years and she could feel the craving rising again in the pit of her soul.

Dangerous.

Startled awake by the phone in her hand, she looked down at the number pushing across the screen. Thankfully, its former owner set it to vibrate, not ring or she was sure it would bring the coven running. One bar for a signal meant there was no chance she could call out. She was amazed she'd gotten the call to Selene out tucked away in the cell. Fates were on her side, finally. Clutching it like a lifeline. she thanked whoever was watching over her right now for giving her the peace of mind to hold on to it. Standing, she wobbled a little, but felt a bit stronger, at least. A left turn would take her back into the heart of the coven. Looking right, she had no idea where it led, but she'd take her chances and the opportunity for more time to gain her strength back. Holding the wall to keep her steady, she moved further into the hallway. Suddenly she was standing at the junction of three paths. Turning in a circle, she saw only darkness in each direction. No landmarks, no directions and no visible markings gave AJ no idea which way led her out and home to Clarissa. Peering into each hallway, a cool breeze lightly caressed her face, blowing wisps of hair out of her face. That meant an open door or window down the hallway to the left and she hurried in that direction, hoping she was making the right choice.

Chapter Twenty-eight

The last few minutes sitting in front of the club were silent. Selene and Clarissa were lost in their own thoughts. Selene knew Clarissa worried about AJ and she contemplated the darkness that seemed to be invading her. Selene would need to make a drastic change and soon or she would be relegated to the darkness forever.

"That was AJ on the phone earlier," Selene dropped the bomb, waiting for the explosion she knew would follow.

"What?"

"She said she tried to call your phone and left a message."

"Why didn't she ask to talk to me?"

"She's on her way home. She didn't sound good, but she said De Marcus is on his way to find you and I should take you to the club."

"What do you mean she didn't sound good? Is she hurt?"

"Don't know."

"Well why the fuck didn't you ask?"

"Calm down, Clarissa. You and I both know that AJ does what she wants. She was at the coven."

"What? Are you fucking kidding me?"

"This is why she didn't want to talk to you. I'm sure she'll explain things when she gets back."

"You lied to me, Selene. You said it was a friend."

Clarissa yanked her phone from the charging unit.

"Sometimes you have to lie to protect." Selene was unapologetic. Clarissa would have to understand that to protect her, Selene would do whatever it took to keep her safe. It wasn't negotiable. She owed it to AJ.

Selene could hear the message AJ left Clarissa. The instructions were different than what AJ had told her, so there might be a fight when they got to the club.

"AJ said I should go to the penthouse–"

"We're not going to the penthouse, Clarissa. She told me to take you to the club, it's much safer there than trying to get you inside the penthouse."

"Why would she say to go to the penthouse then?" Clarissa listened to the message again.

"The situation obviously changed. You heard her on the phone with me, I know you did."

Clarissa was quiet. She touched the face of the phone with AJ's picture as the background image.

"Look, I know you want me to take you to the penthouse, but AJ wants us to go the club. Besides, I can protect you better there." Selene knew there wasn't a choice in the matter and even if it had been up to her, she still wouldn't let Clarissa go to the penthouse.

"Fine, then we go to the club. That's where she'll be looking for us." Clarissa acquiesced.

"Thanks."

"For what?" Clarissa looked out the window.

"For not making me be the bad guy."

"Oh, you don't need my help for that. You have a *lock* on bad girl, trust me you've got it down pat."

"You might be right." All Selene wanted was a drink, a shower and quiet. At least until AJ got there and then the shit could hit the proverbial fan. Tapping the button for the garage door, she waited until it was just high enough to clear her coup and then slowly drove through, watching her rearview mirror for any strays that might try to follow her in. She wouldn't put it past De Marcus to case her place and AJ's, but Selene had patrols on the perimeter around the clock.

"I want to sit here for a few minutes and catch my breath." Selene tilted the steering wheel up and leaned against the head rest. "I'm tired, Clar. I'm so tired."

"I know you are, honey." She felt Clarissa pat her hand, just as she dozed off.

❦ ❦ ❦ ❦

Jerking, Selene sat up. "How long have I been out? Christ, why did you let me fall a sleep?"

"You need to rest. You're practically walking in your sleep."

"We can't sit in the car. It isn't safe." Selene rubbed her eyes and tried to stretch in the cramped space.

"Who would think to look for us sitting in a car, in the parking lot, Selene? I can't think of a safer place."

"We're like sitting ducks here."

"Relax, we're fine." Clarissa rubbed Selene's hand reassuringly.

Selene was pretty sure Clarissa had been watching the parking lot for AJ. Yet, she hadn't showed up. Selene hoped that wasn't bad news, considering AJ had admitted to being at the coven. Butch was a bastard and if De Marcus was involved, it wasn't good.

Selene pushed her door open and practically spilled onto the floor. Her long frame made it difficult to unfold out of the car. *Why don't I drive an SUV like everyone else?* She thought as she stretched to her full length.

She held the elevator door for Clarissa. "After you."

Clarissa's thin smile let her know she wasn't thrilled with the change in plans. A few more minutes and she would be sipping a drink, planning how to get De Marcus, and waiting for AJ. Even she didn't know how long that would take, so best to settle in for the next few hours.

"Boss," Jax said when he spotted her exiting the elevator.

"Shit." She realized she'd pushed the club button and not the button for her private floor. It was habit to hit the club first to check things out. "Jax."

"Clarissa, how are you? You look beautiful." Jax walked casually to Selene and Clarissa.

"Hello again, Jax." Clarissa started to take the offered hand, but it was quickly withdrawn.

Jax opted instead for a kiss to the cheek. "Great to see you again, Love. To what do we owe this visit so soon?

Selene watched the exchange between the two, and if she didn't know better she would say Jax had a crush on Clarissa. Good thing AJ wasn't there, he'd be carrying his head in his hands right about now.

"Jax, I want you to take Clarissa downstairs and make sure she stays safe."

"Is there a problem?" Concern laced his voice.

"Nothing I can't handle."

"You got it." He turned to Clarissa and said, "It

would be my pleasure to watch over this delicate little flower."

"Hold up there, Don Juan." Selene whispered in his ear. "If you lay a finger on her, you'll lose it and probably the hand that it's attached to, so don't touch."

"No worries," Jax said. Before he left he tossed his head towards the club. "I think you better check out the club, got a few visitors you might want to see."

Selene surveyed the crowded room, the men were three thick at the bar and the testosterone was flying as each of the guys tried to outdo the rest with his leather, his pocket swag, or the variety of metal accoutrements sticking out in various places, be it face, clothing or skin.

"Who are you talking about?" Selene turned only to find Jax and Clarissa gone. "Great."

Selene felt like she'd lost a day somewhere finding herself exactly where she was only the day before. She and Clarissa had talked in the car for hours, debating where they should wait for AJ and then there was the meeting Ian and now back to the club. Time, while fleeting always seemed to slip past Selene. She need to sleep, rest her mind and meditate on what she would do next.

Selene walked to the bar and held up two fingers to the bartender who nodded in acknowledgement. Her mind was with Clarissa and Jax as she took a sip of her drink. While she knew she didn't have anything to worry about, being on guard wasn't something she could turn off. She knew if De Marcus wanted to enter the club, he'd find a way or send in a patsy to case the place. Maybe he already had. She had no way of knowing but better to assume it had happened than be surprised.

She hated nights like this, the smell of sweaty men looking to get lucky with either gender made for a rougher than normal crowd sometimes. Not necessarily physically rough, *but the peacock are pruning*, she thought as she watched the men jockey for positions around the available women in the bar. The show had ended over an hour ago, but the effects were lasting.

The Bears in leather harnesses and pants, stalked the room. Tops looking for bottoms. Patrons flagging their particular fetish, mixed with vanilla's just in the club to see what all the fuss was about. Fewer women populated the regular nights, opting for the newbie and ladies nights. Selene had constructed the ladies nights as a safe zone where women could experience the scene without the hawkish nature men brought to the club. A huge success she was proud of deep down inside, though she wouldn't voice it to anyone.

Making her way upstairs to a better vantage point, she pushed through the stinky, sweating leathers with hard-ons. A man who didn't know better slapped her ass as she passed by. In a flash she turned with a growl, grabbed him by the throat, and pushed his up against another man.

"If you put your hands on another woman without her permission, I'll rip your throat out. Got it?" Selene let her fingers dig gently into his soft skin. The urge to snap his neck had to be controlled, so she pushed him back against his buddies. They stared in amazement watching Selene pick him up off his feet just a few inches. "Understand?"

Her grip barely allowed him to nod his acceptance.

"Good, now get the fuck out of my club."

Setting him down, her eyes could've bored a hole right through him. Selene smiled at the hum surrounding him when she walked away. She liked it when men underestimated her. She liked it even more when she could put them in their place. It wasn't men she hated, just assholes and she hadn't met many who weren't.

Climbing the stairs to her lair, she passed couples in various stages of intimacy. Finally, she had to tap one couple who would get her license revoked if they went much further.

"Get a room, this isn't going to happen out here in the hall," Selene whispered in the man's ear.

He turned and glared at her, then his eyes went wide in the realization of who told her to move on. He was a regular, who knew her by reputation and he did exactly as he was instructed. Grabbing his liaison's hand, he pulled her with him so fast the poor woman practically stumbled in his haste to get away from the menace Selene imposed. Closing the door to her private vantage point, she turned her attention to the floor below. She hated babysitting the crowd, but Jax had alluded that someone she knew was out there. Craning her neck through the window that enclosed the office she looked to her left across the floor—nothing. Turning right—still nothing. Just before pulling herself back into the office, she caught sight of platinum blond hair.

Francesca danced below her. A brunette swayed around her and then turned and flirted with a dark haired man positioned so close their bodies shared a passing glance. The brunette turned back around and let her body flirt with Francesca again.

Something inside Selene wanted to possess

Francesca again, but if she did Francesca would never experience life the same, see it the same way or live it alive as she knew it today. She owned Francesca, or did Francesca own her? Selene wished she'd hadn't taken Francesca's virginity. They would forever be linked through blood, a weaker, but similar bond to what Clarissa and AJ shared. Virginal blood was that potent. Staying her distance would keep Francesca an innocent heart. Selene detached from her emotions, it was better that way for both of them.

Friendship wasn't an option either. Selene's friendships were all superficial, surface level and nothing beyond skin deep. She didn't have intimate, lingering moments. This was her creed. The heart attaches to nothing leaving no room for pain. She'd live long past those relationships. Filling the void with a temporary fix filled the void just long enough to stop the cravings. But all cravings returned. So did the void.

The crowded room pulsed with the music, the thumping, pounding vibrations became almost primal as the dancers swayed against each other. Without knowing, someone watching the experience for the first time would assume it was a ritualistic, cultural dance culminating in a mass mating cabal. Selene's palms were sweating, her heart raced, but she couldn't turn away from the vision. Francesca was throwing off pheromones like crazy. Anyone in the vicinity was being hit with them and Selene was hyper-sensitive to Francesca after their last experience together. That sacred virginal blood had sealed their fates. Selene scanned the crowd and picked up something from a man standing off on the periphery of the crowd. He was laser-focused on Francesca and started to thread his way through the crowd straight for her. The hair on the back of Selene's neck stood. *Danger*. She didn't pick up any vampire vibes off the guy. He was a drunk with one thing on his mind, *her* Francesca. He stood behind an unsuspecting Francesca, grabbed her arm, and spun her around. He wrapped her in an embrace and tried to kiss her. The crowd eased back, sensing a moment was about to happen. They clapped, egging the man on, as his hands traveled around Francesca's body. *Kiss, kiss, kiss*. Francesca tried to push him off, but in his drunken state, it was like pushing pudding around with a spoon.

Selene launched herself through the window, landing behind the man. The crowd widened, giving her more room to work on the asshole. As she grabbed his arm, she kicked him behind the knee to knock him backwards. Wrapping her arm around his neck as he fell, she choked him out and dropped him to the floor. At the snap of her fingers, a giant of a man quickly ran to her and slung the drunk over his shoulder.

"Get his ass out of here."

"You got it boss." He lumbered off the dance floor and out the front door.

"Selene," Francesca whispered, rubbing her arm. "Are you hurt?"

Selene's gaze roamed over Francesca, looking for any sign of a bruise. Her mind raced in Francesca's presence. Every thought consumed by doing exactly what the drunk had done, only with a little more finesse.

"Well, who do we have here?" The brunette from earlier butted in, and stood next to Francesca.

"Oh, um, Daphne, Selene. Selene, Daphne." Francesca stared at Selene.

"Nice to meet you, I've heard so much about you.

You've made quite an impression on my friend and I can see why. Very heroic, jumping down from up there. Are you okay?" Daphne had the clear sense to stay where she was, Selene noticed.

"I'm quite fine, thank you." Selene turned her attention towards Francesca. Her mind could only focus on her want, her need to be close to Francesca. "Are you okay?"

"Thank you, I'm fine," Francesca colored with embarrassment as Selene's fingertips ran down her arms.

It was an intimate moment shared on a crowded dance floor. The crowd started its routine again, ignoring the three women standing in the center.

"Well, I'll just leave you ladies to your dancing. Sorry to interrupt."

Without another word, Selene turned and pushed her way off the dance floor. If she stayed any longer and she would scoop Francesca off to her room and change both their lives forever.

"Hey, you're not going to just let her get away are you? She's a hottie, girl."

Selene heard Daphne whisper the encouragement, which only caused her to speed up her pace to the back.

A tap on Selene's shoulder stopped her, but she didn't turn around. She didn't have to. She knew who was behind her. Francesca.

❧ ❧ ❧ ❧

Francesca stood close enough to Selene to smell her, and a flash back to their last time together unsettled her instantly. She wanted to reach out and pull her back, hell she just wanted to touch her.

"Selene..." Something in the air felt odd. The tension was laced with electricity and excitement. Each woman stood almost frozen by the contact, afraid to move forward and break the contact or turn and face what each knew they wanted. "Can we talk, please?" Francesca's voice trembled.

"I don't think that's a good idea, do you?"

"Actually, I don't know what's happening to me. I'm captivated by you like I've never been captivated by someone before. I can't seem to get you out of my mind. I mean...well...I just mean that I've been thinking and wondering if—"

"Let me save you the trouble," Selene said, turning towards Francesca pulling her out of the flow of traffic through the club. "What happened last night can't happen—"

Francesca moved closer to Selene, unable to control her thoughts, her body, she raised up on the tips of her toes and pulled Selene down for a kiss. Her mouth opened slightly, the tip of her tongue flicked out and traced Selene's lips. Selene lifted her off her feet and grabbed her so tight she thought she might pass out. Light-headed from the contact, she fell deeper into the kiss. Their tongues dueled and their hands gripped more tightly. Francesca felt somehow as if Selene was giving her a last kiss. The urgency couldn't be denied and yet she wasn't letting go, not yet.

Feeling her feet on the floor, Francesca pulled back slightly and looked down. All reason inside shattered, replaced by desire, lust or whatever made someone want another so badly they would do anything to have them. These emotions were unfamiliar to Francesca. Her logical mind told her to step back and walk—no run away, but that part of her mind was slowly receding. Urgency took over.

Selene tipped her chin up and their eyes met. From the deep recesses of her mind she could almost hear Selene warning her off, while Selene reached around and pressed Francesca's hips against her own. The gentle pressure sent a spike of pleasure from Francesca's clit to her nipples, each hardening at the contact. Suddenly feeling lightheaded, she rested her head on Selene's shoulder and took a slow, deep breath. Scent brought back memories again.

"I'm sorry," Francesca whispered as she pushed her hand under Selene's coat and stroked her ribs.

With a quick intake of breath, Selene pulled Francesca tighter against her body. Responding to the signal as permission, Francesca slid her hand under Selene's shirt to glide around her back, pulling her closer, too. She slipped her hand down and felt a firm, round ass flinch under her touch. Her only thought, press on.

Suddenly she was lifted off her feet again. Selene grabbed her ass and pulled Francesca up on to her hips and wound Francesca's legs around her waist. Without thinking Francesca lifted her face, closed her eyes and waited for the kiss she knew was coming. Trying to steel her body even if only for a moment, she wanted to be in control of the situation as it unfolded. That was an exercise in futility, because the moment their lips met Francesca was gone. Francesca's arms wrapped around Selene's shoulders steadying her body, as Selene rocked her against her hard stomach. Selene growled, pushing her into a dark corner against the wall. Francesca felt teeth graze her neck and jerked her body against Selene's, taking her further into the darkness that enveloped them both.

"You have no idea what your messing with, Francesca," Selene said, a husky tone giving Francesca goose bumps.

"I want to…I want to know you…" Francesca threaded her fingers in Selene's hair and forced her lower. A flick of her nipple caused a sharp intake of breath. She was so far gone she didn't know when Selene had pushed her shirt up and unhooked her bra, exposing her for Selene's pleasure.

"There may be no going back, Francesca."

The warning went unheeded as Francesca begged for more. A door opened and she was on Selene's desk, again. Her mind spinning with all the endorphins, she begged for more, more mouth, more touching and more…

Things crashed around her as she felt Selene step away. Suddenly cold and shocked, Francesca reached up and covered her breasts. Standing only a foot away Selene looked like a wild animal. Her eyes red and remote, her hair tussled and uncontrolled, Selene seemed more feline than human as she crawled towards Francesca.

"I warned you, Francesca. I tried to tell you that we wouldn't be good together, but you've sealed us together with your innocence, your virginal blood. My kind of darkness isn't for your kind." Selene's tone was foreboding, ominous.

"My kind? I don't understand, Selene." Francesca felt like she should be afraid, but something inside her embraced this dark Selene. She didn't fall for the *bad girl* type. It didn't intrigue her. Selene was something else though. All she wanted was for Selene to own her, to take her.

Fangs popped, Selene started to morph in to her heightened state and all Francesca could do was watch as it happened. Waves of sexual tension buffeted Francesca's body as Selene stalked closer. Finally towering over Francesca, she reached up and caressed Selene's face, her fingers rubbed her lips open and she touched a fang.

❧❧❧❧

Selene froze at the touch. Instead of being scared, Francesca's fingers opened her lips and touched one fang and then the other. Selene practically melted when Francesca licked her lips and pulled Selene down to kiss her. Her body arched at the contact, Francesca pulled her on top of her body and begged her to touch her.

"You're not surprised, scared?"

"You're like AJ and AJ doesn't scare me. Why should you?"

Pulling back she felt Francesca wrap herself around her body stopping her from standing up, Selene growled. "You've been with AJ?"

Francesca rested on her elbows, clearly shocked by the accusation. "No, AJ has a girlfriend. Why would I be with AJ?"

"How do you know about AJ then?" Selene leaned back, putting more distance between them. Her mind raced at what Francesca had said. How could Francesca possibly know AJ was a vampire? Why wasn't she afraid? Everyone was afraid of her kind, everyone. Her body ached for release, but this new information was like a cold shower to her body. It shook and cramped as it rolled back into its human form.

Selene unwrapped Francesca's legs from her waist and stumbled backwards to the couch. She ran her fingers through her hair, pulling her braid from behind her and flicking the end, something she did when she was perplexed. Her mind felt like it was recovering from a hangover. Dropping her head back, her world spun until she closed her eyes. Filling her lungs with a deep breath, she suddenly had Francesca straddling her lap, her warm breath on her face.

"Tell me what is happening to me, Selene." Francesca forced Selene to face her. "I can't stop thinking about you. I think about fucking you, I dream about it, my body aches for your touch. What's going on?"

Selene could barely look at Francesca. She suddenly wanted to put as much distance between them as possible. Even though Francesca knew what she was, she wouldn't be deterred. She couldn't scare Francesca into silence. In fact, the exact opposite, Francesca clung to her like a wet T-shirt, exposing Selene to the world, at least Francesca's world.

"My skin craves your fingers on it. I want–"

"Silence." Selene tried to stand, but Francesca pushed her back into the couch.

Her shirt was ripped open, buttons scattering everywhere. Francesca craned her neck down and let her tongue glide over Selene's neck. Sliding off her lap and kneeling on the floor, Francesca attacked her stomach with little bites and then licked the nips. Pulling at the belt around Selene's waist, she opened her jeans and tried to pull them off.

"Lift," Francesca commanded. She narrowed her eyes with a sexy smoldering gaze that nearly sent

Selene over the edge. Selene's thoughts ricocheted around trying to make sense of the sudden twist of fate.

Chapter Twenty-nine

The dark hallway seemed to go on forever. The only saving grace was the gentle breeze that still blew in AJ's face. Her legs were heavy and she still struggled to stay upright. Her focus to keep moving was seeing Clarissa's face and killing De Marcus. Squinting, she thought she could see light further down the hallway. Finally, she'd be out of the hellhole and on her way home. Footfalls made her stop. Someone was behind her, but she wasn't sure if they were in the same tunnel, or if it was just echoes traveling down the three separate hallways. She slipped against the wall, knowing if someone were following, her outline would stand out against the backdrop of the light.

Staying close to the rough cement wall, AJ tried to pick up the pace. She became winded the more she exerted, pushing herself harder meant expending more energy and her body just wasn't ready for the taxing getaway.

"Shh, hear that?"

AJ's ears picked up a voice behind her, freezing she held her breath.

"Naw, I don't hear anything," a male voice said.

"I heard something. I know that bitch is down here, where else could she be? She was practically dead."

"Did you see, Sherman? She did a pretty good

job on his wrists. Drained him…" Fingers snapped together. "Like that, I betcha. Besides, look what she did to Butch. Bashed his head in and cut it off."

"Yeah, that's why we have to find her. Who's gonna take over the coven. I mean, De Marcus? I heard he's been angling to be high lord."

The voices faded away from AJ but they'd at least let her know that Butch was dead and they were after her. The coven was rudderless. That didn't mean the boat couldn't float, it would just take a while for the next leader to step up and take it. God only knew who that would be and how much of a blood bath would have to happen before a leader was declared. The ascension to power was never easy for vampires, at least not at the coven. She'd seen it at least a dozen times since she'd been turned. Men still dominated the hierarchy due to their sheer numbers. While there were women in the coven, the old ways still existed at some level. Men turned men in greater numbers than women. Women were seen as members of their master's harems. Breaking free of the tyrannical hold was hard for women. Vampires had an innate need to belong to a family structure. It's what kept them together through thick and thin. Women were oppressed and men maintained control of their family's futures. Basically, the coven in a nutshell.

Reaching into her pocket she pulled out the cell phone she still had, and a few capsules. Breaking one, she shoved it under her tongue and rested against the cold wall. The time on the phone told her that sunrise would be in a few hours. Then what was the light streaming in ahead of her? Moving closer, she heard water moving and suddenly she was sloshing ankle deep in sludge. Stepping further, the water rose to her knees, but the light was still significantly further down the tunnel. Backpedalling, she stepped out of the wet and flung herself on the ground.

"Could this night get any worse?"

Voices.

"I just had to ask, didn't I?" She slid her body back against the wall. "Why didn't I take the right tunnel?"

More voices, this time edging closer to her location. She needed to make a choice. She wasn't in any shape to fight it out with whoever was coming down the tunnel, but she didn't want to have to swim if she could avoid it. Looking up she noticed the dark recesses above the opening. It was still a ways down, but she could either hide in the freezing water, or hope she had the strength to suspend herself above the opening. The pitch-black darkness of the corners would keep her hidden until she assessed the situation. Then there was the possibility that the opening was just that, an opening to the outside. AJ shook her head. Butch would have had all accesses to the coven sealed or locked down to prevent any possibility of trespassers getting in by accident.

Voices came closer.

She needed to act fast. Pushing herself up, she waded into the water. Her body shivered instantly, the water stunk and the cold was biting. Apropos, AJ thought, the biting cold reference for a vampire. The bottom dropped off suddenly and her feet slipped off the edge. Now she was treading water. The opening was closed off by bars dropping into the water. She'd have no leverage to launch herself up into the corner, so she was stuck in the water. Turning around she tried to focus on the voices coming closer. She could make out two, maybe three men moving towards her. She swam back into the corner opposite of the lit opening. The light would blind the men and hopefully scan right past her, but she couldn't take any chances.

The phone and capsules in her pocket!

Shit!

Reaching into her pocket she passed the phone and grabbed the few capsules she had left. Without thinking, she popped them in her mouth. *Yuck.* Whatever was in the water was now in her mouth. *Shit.* She didn't have a choice. Lose the blood supply or take what she had and hope for the best. He body wasn't functioning normally and all the capsules she'd taken in the last few hours should have put her in a blood hangover. Her body needed all she could handle right now or she wouldn't be able to defend herself if trouble came knocking.

"See anything, Sherman?"

"I told you last time I didn't see anything, asshole."

"Look closer, she's gotta be down her somewhere. I could smell her back there. I'm sure of it."

"You sure you weren't smelling that shit you stepped on in that other tube?"

"Silence you morons. Listen." An authoritative voice commanded.

"I don't hear anything but Sherman farting."

A gurgling sound pierced the silence. Mr. Authority was probably strangling the smartass. AJ knew the type well. Chances are Mr. Authority was vying for high lord, and his ace in the hole was her. If he brought her back he could challenge anyone who had any thought of moving on the position.

"Shuuut-uuuup," he hissed. A thud sounded,

someone landed on the ground. "Check out the water."

"I ain't goin' in there. There are snakes, bugs and shit floating around in there." Sherman protested.

AJ felt herself gag at the new information. Sliding a hand over her mouth, she bit the side of her lip, letting blood fill her mouth mixing with the capsules under her tongue. She hoped it would amp the dose and mix quicker into her system.

"There…did you hear that? Get your ass in that water and check it out. If you don't, you're going in, just not coming out. Get my drift?" Mr. Authority threatened the two men.

"Fine. You first, Sherman." His voice squeaked out. Obviously he was the one Mr. Authority grabbed by the throat.

"Both of you get your asses in there."

"Fine," they said in unison.

AJ retreated into the corner, ready to submerge in the dirty water if she needed to. She couldn't fight the two men, so she'd have to outwit them. The light was behind and to her side, so she could see them clearly as they waded into the water. Each man moved so slow she was sure their leader would push them in and as if on cue he pushed them face first into the water with his foot.

"Hurry-up and get your asses in there."

Standing and spiting mouthfuls of water, the men growled at Mr. Authority.

"Asshole," one whispered.

Wading out deeper into the water, AJ kept an eye on them as they split up and went to the side of the catch-bowl. Moving along the wall, they waved their arms into the center hoping to catch something. One of them edged closer. AJ knew her only option would be to go under and stay submerged until he'd passed. Looking around she searched for something to use as a weapon. Anything would do. Remembering the cell phone in her pocket, she pulled it out and flipped it open, nothing. Slipping under the water, she could see just enough through the green murky muck to see the man close the distance between them. Swimming towards the center of the water, she tapped the man on the leg as he passed by. It was enough to send the man screaming back towards Mr. Authority.

"Something touched my leg. I felt it."

"Get your ass back in there."

"Fuck you, I told you there were probably snakes in there and I felt one. Hard sombitch hit me on the thigh."

"You want to see if she's in there, then you get your ass in there."

"Puss."

AJ could hear the gruff voice and knew he didn't have balls enough to come into the water. Guys like that delegated to others, but they didn't do dirty work and this was definitely dirty work.

"Hey, Sherman. You got anything?"

"Nope."

"Get yer ass out of there then. We have another tunnel to check out. So let's get busy. We'll burn it. Go back and get a few gas cans and flood this tunnel, then light it up. The smoke'll vent out of that hole right there."

"You got it."

"You got five minutes to get that shit lit up and back over to the other tunnel."

"I can't—"

"Run, asshole."

AJ broke the top of the water just enough to release the breath she was holding. *Asshole.* Her eyes were just above the water, never leaving the retreating backs. The sound of feet hitting cement echoed down the tunnel. She needed to get the hell out of the coven and now.

Chapter Thirty

Francesca knelt before Selene, begging for her pants.

"Off."

"No, explain how you know AJ is a vampire." Selene stood and yanked her arms, pulling her to her feet. "How?"

Francesca tried to pull her arms free, but Selene grabbed tighter each time she jerked back.

"Tell me. How is it you know about her, about me?"

"I was in the lab when Kevin killed himself. I saw..." Francesca paused remembering. He'd committed suicide in the most brutal way, practically decapitating himself. She wanted to run, but AJ and Selene had walked in just as she was going to make a run for it. Her boss had put him in the cold storage box and said it was for safe keeping. Safe keeping for whom? She'd suspected something wasn't right with AJ when she'd done her blood testing for insurance work. Usually Dr. Mayfield ran her tests, but he had gotten busy, so he'd asked her to do the double blind testing on the sample. Double-blind? Who does a double blind on lab work for insurance? When she looked at it under the microscope, the samples were practically vibrating on the slide. Adding the various antigens that insurance companies would test for only made her more suspicious. The blood consumed everything added to it. Repairing itself at such a rapid rate that she was shocked. She would've questioned Dr. Mayfield but he died suddenly, leaving her in charge of the lab. The biggest promotion came with a visit to the boss's office.

"Dr. Swartz, I'm thrilled to have you as Dr. Mayfield's replacement."

"I'm honored you even considered me for the position." Francesca said, nervously standing in front of AJ's desk.

"You were at the top of your class, you come from Thorndike Lab at Harvard Medical Center and your research is impeccable. I'd say we are lucky to have you." AJ stood and walked around her desk, leaning on it in front of Francesca. "I do have some paperwork for you to sign and something to talk to you about though. It might make you rethink taking over Dr. Mayfield's position. So in an effort of full disclosure...."

That was the beginning of her learning about AJ and her blood's ability to aggressively heal itself. She'd been given an out, but her curiosity and the research potential, had cemented her position at Lockwood Pharmaceutical. It was easy to deduce from that point forward who was and who wasn't in AJ's inner circle of vampire friends. She suspected Maggie, AJ's assistant, knew as well, but she would never bring it up in conversation. It wouldn't be polite and she didn't want to be seen as a gossip, so she kept everything she knew and suspected to herself. It was easier that way. But Selene was different. She'd seen Selene in the lab that day with AJ pulling Kevin's body out of the cold box. If it wasn't for the long braid that broke between her shoulder blades, her physique, strength and size gave the impression of a well-built man. When she turned around however, Selene's dark eyes mesmerized Francesca. An old soul was the only thing that she could attribute them too. Hence, it was easy to label Selene as a vampire. She didn't make the connection or recognize Selene until after her visit to the club. She was the same woman, just different somehow. Darkness, mysterious and dangerous were written all over her, now. Then again, maybe it had been there the whole time. She wouldn't know since she never saw Selene after the suicide incident.

"You're hurting me, Selene." The quiver in her voice only added to the tension between them.

Instantly she was released. Selene turned her back, pulling at her shirt, trying to cover herself. Francesca touched her back, a flinch her only response to the touch.

"Selene. I'd apologize but I don't know what I would be apologizing for."

"You don't have anything to apologize for, it's me."

Francesca wrapped herself around Selene's back, hugging her tightly. "Why? You didn't do anything wrong. Last time I checked we were both consenting adults, right?"

"You can't consent when I'm around. I mean I have the ability to…"

"Did you? Did you make me come to you and force me to make love to you?" Francesca said, shocked that she hadn't thought about Selene's abilities to control her. She'd seen the way AJ and Selene seemed to have a connection that day in the office, but she just thought that was an old wives tale. Vampires talking to each other without having to say anything.

"No! Of course not. I saw you and I wanted you,

I just didn't..."

"What? Didn't what?"

"Stop you from coming to me." Selene tried to pull out of the embrace but Francesca held tighter. "That night in the room...I...I purposely took the dom role when I learned it was you. So see, I used my influence to get what I wanted."

"And?"

"And?"

"Yeah, and? What...you showed me something I came here willing to explore. Stop Selene. We were destined to meet. I believe that. I believe in fate. I believe I get to control my own life and right now I want you in that life. Of course that is assuming...that you...I mean..."

"You don't understand. We've shared blood, you've given me your virginity, unknowingly of course, but you won't be able to fight it."

"What if I don't want to fight it?"

"Good thing, because you won't, unless I..."

Chapter Thirty-one

AJ lifted herself out of the muck and grime of the murky water, gagging from the noxious smell. "I need to hose off. Fuck."

Scaling the wall, she reached for any purchase for her fingertips. The cracks and crevices were microscopic in some instances, but enough to allow her to pull her ragged body up. Speed was critical or she risked being discovered by Sherman who would return to make the water a raging inferno. Elbowing her way on to the ledge she peered outside and saw freedom. Rusted through bars barely recognizable as metal practically disintegrated as soon as she touched them.

"At least something is going my way." She whispered, hearing someone running down tunnel.

"Hey, who the fuck...oh shit it's you. Hey, I found her," Sherman screamed to no one.

Waving at the little minion without responding, she slipped down to the outside and landed harder than she'd anticipated. It was dawn, but her eyes still weren't focusing well enough. The tree line was only about a hundred yards. Staying here wasn't an option. Praying her body was up for the challenge, she made a full sprint for the trees. AJ crouched behind a log to catch her breath and listened. She heard yelling in the distance and the whoosh of fire, as the smoke billowed out of the vent.

"You asshole, how are we supposed to follow her now?"

The crunch of decaying leaves under her feet was the only sound in the wooded area. Her mind focused on her escape. She circled around to reach the front of the coven, hoping her car and briefcase would still be there. Getting in could be a problem, but she'd worry about that when the time came. For now, she had to stay hidden because assuming the coven didn't have day walkers would be foolish, if not deadly. Smelling like shit right now had its advantages. Climbing into a tree, she shimmied up into the canopy, hoping for a better vantage point and the opportunity to see where she was in relationship to the coven.

Hugging the trunk she turned around to view the other direction. Trees and the smoke from the fire in the sewer to her left were the only landmarks she could make out. If she remembered correctly, the coven would be in front of her, just off her right shoulder. Something hard pressed against her thigh as she wrapped her leg around the tree to stabilize herself. Gingerly putting her hand in her pocket, she pulled out the cell phone and her tin. The cell phone was useless now and she considered tossing it. Instead, she tucked it back in the pocket. A careless mistake could lead someone right to her. A deep growl suddenly rumbled through the air.

Dogs!

Great.

Chapter Thirty-two

Selene should have been thinking about De Marcus, she knew, but all she could think about, all she could smell was Francesca and her sex. Her body was oozing pheromones and Selene was eating them up like candy. This was the problem being with Francesca, she couldn't think of anything else. Her animal instincts ruled, banishing all duty or reason beyond Francesca. The tight arms wrapped around her, the warm body pressed against her back and the hands slipping beneath her shirt were unraveling her well laid out plan. Now she had to deal with Francesca. Scaring her off wasn't an option, not if she knew about AJ and by default, her. *Fuck!*

"Selene?"

"Francesca, please…"

"Selene, please. Turn around. I'm not leaving, we need to talk."

"I don't think it's talking you want, Francesca."

Turning around was her first mistake. Francesca slid her hands around and pulled her closer. She opened Selene's shirt wider and pressing against her. Selene's nipples pressed against Francesca and she sucked in a breath.

"Tell me you don't want this. Tell me you don't want me."

The dilemma. She could lie, but that would only push her further into the darkness she was trying to escape.

"I wish I could." Francesca pulled Selene's head down for a kiss that was her undoing.

Wetness rushed between her legs. She ripped Francesca's shirt open and pushed her back onto the desk. Oh, she would never be able to work at that desk again, she realized. Her mind raced as she searched out what she wanted, first Francesca's lips, then her breasts and finally ending her search between Francesca's legs. She shredded Francesca's panty hose and hiked her skirt up to her waist. Selene dipped her tongue down and pushed further, past wet lips, into the silky warmth that was Francesca's essence. Her mind went wild, her heart raced and her fingers joined her tongue as she roughly explored what Francesca was willingly offering her. Her fingers threaded through Selene's hair, holding her head in place while Francesca writhed under her lips.

Selene's tongue darted in and out of Francesca, tasting her with each probing stab. She wanted more from Francesca but didn't dare. Finally, Francesca pulled her head away and sat up on the desk, kissing her. Francesca's own tongue mimicked the way Selene had play with her pussy, darting in and out, licking her essence off Selene's lips.

"Show me," Francesca requested.

"What?" Selene wasn't sure what Francesca was asking. Her head floated in the haze of the sexual frenzy and she wanted it to continue.

"I want to see you, the real you. Fangs and all," Francesca said as she kissed Selene's neck. The feel of Francesca's tongue flicking down her neck set her skin ablaze. The contact pushed her over the edge of desire and directly into the path of lust.

"I'm not a magician, Francesca. I don't perform on command, but if you insist…" Selene felt her fangs pop first and then the rest of her body followed suit. Fangs were always the first defense mechanism for a vampire, they protected, punctured and primed when a vampire fought for survival. Taking another's blood was survival as far as a vampire was concerned.

Francesca tapped the tip of her fang and then the other. She followed it with a deep kiss, her tongue purposely grazing the tips drawing her own blood.

Jerking back, Selene slapped her hand over her mouth, as if she doing so would prevent the urge to taste more of Francesca.

Francesca reached up and gently peeled Selene's hand off her face, placing Selene's finger in her mouth. Slowly, seductively she began to suck the tip, her tongue rolling back and forth over it. The action was pushing Selene to the breaking point and she did everything she could to control the vibration that was starting at her clit and moving outward through the rest of her body. Francesca had to know the effect she was having on her body. *Of course she did, she was doing it deliberately and it was getting the desired reaction,* Selene was sure as she looked down into the smoky eyes of her soon to be lover. She was past the point of caring whether Francesca knew what she was doing anymore.

Selene's tongue flicked at Francesca's wrist, feeling the heartbeat racing under the skin. Moving up she sucked on the inside of her elbow, the pulse getting stronger the closer she got to Francesca's heart. She heard the blood gushing in Francesca's veins. *Goosh, goosh, goosh,* each rhythmic heartbeat, a siren call to Selene. Her tongue slicked along a salty trail up

Francesca's neck, while her hand pushed Francesca's legs open and two fingers slipped into her folds. At first she gently suckled the inviting neck, her fingers slipping in and out with the pulse of Francesca's heart. Palming her clit, Selene pulled Francesca back giving her more exposure to Francesca's wanting body. Selene's mouth covered erect nipples, afraid she would accidently bite the soft, pliant skin under her grazing fangs.

"Oh god," Francesca moaned softly, her back curved and relaxed and then arched again as her body released an orgasm. Selene continued to work her hand faster, urging another climax from Francesca.

"Don't stop." Francesca begged, clinging to Selene desperately.

The door banged open and both women froze.

"Selene, I want to go home," Clarissa demanded. "Now. I...oh *shit*."

Chapter Thirty-three

AJ sat in the tree and watched the action below her heat up. Men barked orders, minions trying to follow them, and dogs drowned out those orders with their own barking. Chaos was in full bloom below her and all she could do was laugh internally and watch. Her place in the tree was hopefully high enough and secluded, and if not, there wasn't much she could do. Moving would risk exposure and that wasn't an option. Her hand clutched the tin of capsules. She hadn't had the time to open it when the dogs alerted her to the new threat.

She hoped her shit bath was enough to cover her scent from the dogs, but it was a long shot. Pressing into the tree trunk, she remained perfectly still. Patience was what she needed, besides it would give her the time to regenerate and build-up her strength. With every passing minute she felt her body getting stronger. Her thoughts went to Clarissa, how she missed her lover. A day, a night was too long to be apart when they hadn't been without each other longer than a day since reconciling. They woke up together and slept in the same house, sometimes in separate rooms due to AJ's schedule, but still together. She was sure Clarissa must be frantic, but there was absolutely nothing she could do right now to calm her lover. In her weakened state, AJ's ability to connect with Clarissa was more difficult. She could get Clarissa's thoughts, but she had more difficulty pushing hers to Clarissa. They would need to be a lot closer if she wanted to reach Clarissa and put her at ease.

"Let's go, she's going to get further away if we don't move," bossy man from earlier screamed.

The small group of searchers moved en mass away from the coven and deeper into the forested land. AJ waited what seemed like hours, yet she knew it was probably only minutes at most. Her mind worked out the logistics of getting to her car, assuming it was still where she parked it, getting off the coven grounds unseen and back to Clarissa. She needed to protect her lover. De Marcus was evil and he would be out to eliminate everyone around Clarissa, keeping her to himself for eternity. Scrambling down from her perch, she zigzagged from tree to tree, trying to stay covered while weaving her way back to the coven parking. Her car still sat on the small hill where she'd parked it. Little did she realize at the time, parking it facing down the drive would be convenient. Searching the lot, she didn't see anyone around it. No sounds caught her attention. She crept closer, keeping low to stay hidden. It was eerily quiet—almost too quiet. Scanning the grounds, she suspected the impending dawn would keep the majority of the coven in lock down. All she had to worry about were the few out scouting for her.

Crawling to the side of her car, she reached up into the wheel well and felt around for the replacement box she always placed on her rental. She'd learned a long time ago, that rental agencies took their sweet time sending a replacement key, and time sometimes wasn't her friend. Staying alive in a world that wanted you dead meant planning was a necessity. It had kept her alive more times than she could remember. She'd built her life around possibilities, usually of the worst kind. The metal box slid, dropping its contents into her hand, a key and a small wad of cash. No use in having a car, if you couldn't keep it filled with gas. Sliding down the fender she slipped the key into the door lock, turned it and waited, worried the sound of the lock turning might bring someone running.

Nothing.

She slipped into the driver's seat and gently pulled the door closed. Pushing the lock button, she leaned across the seat and waited again. Her heart raced, anxiety coursed through her. It was difficult to stay focused. Suddenly her mind bounced from the past to the present. Clarissa then and her lover now flashed through her thoughts. How could she have not known Clarissa was alive all those decades? Why didn't she search for AJ? Why was self-doubt eating at her now? AJ closed her eyes and pushed all of the questions from her mind. Now wasn't the time to linger on pointless regrets.

She slipped the key into the ignition and turned it. The car didn't start. Pushing the brake she shifted the car into neutral, slowly let the car roll down the driveway. AJ peeked over the dash and then all around her, still nothing. She would only get one chance to get out and off the mountain, so she needed to be quick. Without power the car would be difficult to steer, so she prepared to start the engine before she careened off the road into a tree. She cranked the SUV and it lurched into drive as she pushed the gas to the floor.

The back glass shattered with the sound of gunshots, followed by another that splintered the right side of the windshield into webs that nearly blocked her view. She was out of options. *Time to move.* Pushing the SUV harder she slid through the turns. A gun-wielding man raised his weapon and got off a shot that shattered her window. She felt the bullet zip past her face, missing by inches.

All AJ could think was move faster. *Faster!* She heard yelling behind her, but at the speed she was moving there was no way they would catch her on foot. Not even vampires could run that fast. A splattering of bullets rained across the back end of the SUV before it was finally silent. Hitting the main road, she pushed the car further trying to put as much distance between her and the coven as possible. She'd have to dump the SUV and find another ride to the airport, but anything on the road would be obvious. What she wouldn't do for a phone right now, just to hear Clarissa's voice and know she was safe. She needed that small assurance more than she needed to breathe. Maybe she could find a pay phone somewhere. Finally passing a strip mall she drove along the front, searching. Nothing, not even a stump, she'd take anything. Asking to use a phone inside was out of the question. She smelled like an outhouse and looked like she'd been dunked in one, too. Gazing down at her hands she felt her gag reflex start. *Keep it together*, she whispered repeatedly.

She pulled behind a row of buildings. Slowing, she surveyed her options of the few cars available: a sedan, a truck and an old Dodge Dart. *Great, not much to choose from.* She pulled into a parking space next to the Dart, figuring it would be the easiest to steal. The Dart would also draw the least amount of attention. The only question was would it make it to the airport fifteen miles away?

Jumping out of the vehicle, AJ grimaced in pain.

Grabbing her side, she felt a something sharp stab her hand. A rib poked through. With all the metal and glass flying around she wasn't surprised she was hit. What surprised her was that she didn't even feel the bullet hit her side—at least she assumed it was a bullet. Today just wasn't her day. Hell, it wasn't even her week if truth be told. She didn't need to lose any more blood. She was running on a deficit as it was. Now it was imperative that she get to the airport and home. If she was going to die she wanted it to be next to Clarissa and not on some deserted Hicksville street. Stepping over to the Dodge, she elbowed the back window, pulled the door lock and slipped into the driver's seat. Reaching underneath she yanked on the wiring harness and pulled two wires. Touching the bare ends made the connection and the engine cranked over. Pumping the gas, she tapped them again and the car started instantly. Slamming the car door, she slid down into the seat, punched the gas and tore out of the parking lot. Slowing just enough to make sure no one was coming down the street, she pulled out on to the main road again and tried to act as local as possible.

She passed the airport sign within minutes, and soon drifted to a stop next to her waiting plane. It wouldn't be long now before she was home and with Clarissa. Her only hope was that Selene would keep her safe.

"Ms. Lockwood, are you all right?"

Those were the last words AJ heard before she collapsed at the stairs of the plane.

Chapter Thirty-four

Clarissa froze, her eyes locked on the scene playing out on top of Selene's desk. She wished she'd knocked now, but what was done was done. She wanted to go home, but knew that Selene wouldn't allow her to be that easy of a target. Her house had a security system, but not much more than that, so she'd wait for AJ at the penthouse.

"I'm sorry, I didn't realize you were otherwise detained, Selene. I'll wait for you next door."

"Sorry boss, she got away from…" Jax stood frozen behind Clarissa, too. "Well, I can see you're—"

Clarissa closed the door before he could finish his sentence. "I think we should give them some privacy, don't you?"

"Well—"

"Really? Have you no shame?"

"No, not really," Jax said following Clarissa back to Selene's room.

"Why am I not surprised, Jax? As you can see Selene is busy, so I'd like you to take me home."

"No can do, Clarissa. Selene told me to keep an eye on you and keep you safe in here." He swept his arm wide, waiting for her to go back inside.

Clarissa's frustration boiled over. "Take me home now, Jax." Clarissa's anger could prompt her to change into a vampire and she was close to ascending into her sub-human form. "Now."

Jax morphed into the most gruesome vampire Clarissa had seen. His soul had to be hundreds of years old. It's withered old frame, with its craggy creases and deep-set eyes stopped Clarissa cold. Her transformation halted. Never had she seen someone look so wicked and dangerous.

"You shouldn't push people, Clarissa. Some of us aren't as nice as AJ or Selene. Now sit the fuck down and wait. Selene will be here when she's finished." Jax's heel caught the door and it slammed behind him. "What's wrong? Surprised?"

"Sorta," she lied. She was shocked. "How old are you Jax?"

"How old is dirt?" He joked. "I've seen things that history books talk about. I've been places you could only dream of and yet, I feel as young as I did when I was brought over."

Clarissa could believe his boastful claims. Old souls like him were rare. She'd never met one, but had heard of the *legends*. They had legendary status amongst the younger bloods. Hard to kill, even harder to find. Their wisdom ran deep, their voices just as so. The fact that he was in Selene's employ was surprising. She suddenly felt safe sitting in the same room with him.

"Your master must–"

"Is long dead. He wasn't worth the time it took to kill him, he gave me a gift I would gladly return if I could."

Clarissa craned her neck as if doing so would encourage him to elaborate further. He didn't bite, instead he sat changing back into his more visually appealing image. Clarissa blew out a breath through pursed lips. She wouldn't get anywhere with Jax, so she might as well relax and wait.

Chapter Thirty-five

Icy fingers spread through the room. Clarissa's interruption had more than dropped the temperature, it had been like jumping into a cold shower with all your clothes on as far as Francesca was concerned. Selene pulled back, clutching at the fragments of her shirt, pulling it closed. Turning away from Francesca, she cinched her belt and poured two fingers of something into a glass.

"Want some?" Her cold tone left little question about how she was feeling.

Francesca knew she should be embarrassed at being caught *in the act,* but her body still ached for Selene. For the third time with Selene she felt as if a job was half-completed.

"No, I'm good. Thanks."

"I'll have Jax take you home." Still with her back to Francesca she shot the drink and then slammed it on the bar and refilled it.

"I don't need Jax to take me home. I need you to talk to me. I need…I don't know what I need…I mean I do know what I need, but clearly that ship has sailed." Francesca pushed down her skirt.

"Your friend was escorted home, so I want to make sure you get home safe."

"Well that's very gallant of you, Selene."

Raising her glass in salute, Selene downed another and then one more. Francesca suspected Selene's metabolism would burn up the alcohol like a Bunsen burner. A hot flame short lived once the gas was turned off.

"I try."

"Yes, I'm sure you do." Francesca straightened her blouse. "We both know that we can't stay away from each other now. I don't know what you've done to me, but I can feel you inside me."

Selene turned to face Francesca and grabbed her arms. "I'm not girlfriend material, Francesca. I'm—"

"Oh, I know, you have that dark, dangerous bitch down. Trust me." Francesca yanked her arms out of Selene's grasp. "I'm a big girl and I know exactly what you are, but trust me I'm not afraid of you."

"You should be."

Selene flung herself down on the couch and let out a deep breath. Francesca couldn't let her off that easy. Selene had done something to her. She didn't feel like her normal self anymore. She hadn't felt normal since her first visit to The Dungeon.

"So it ends before it ever starts? Jesus, I'm sounding like a fucking stalker girlfriend who doesn't get a call back after the first date."

Selene just sat there, staring off and unable to make eye contact. Francesca suspected this wasn't her first time breaking a heart or two and she was sure it wouldn't be her last. Shaking herself, she wondered how she'd gotten so sideways so easily. Her logical mind was starting to fire-up and reason was boiling to the top of her scattered thoughts. Direct contact with Selene had a clouding effect on her, she suspected. Grabbing her jacket and shoes, Francesca could only feel pity for Selene. It was clear she was struggling with her demons. She supposed in a life this long, it was bound to happen.

Francesca's only option was to take back whatever control she had innocently handed over to Selene. While she'd never had addictive tendencies, she suspected breaking away from Selene would feel like withdrawal. *God, what was she thinking?* She barely knew the woman and here she was planning how to deal with dependency. *Christ*, she needed to get as far away from Selene as she could. She'd quit Lockwood Pharmaceuticals! She'd find a new job! Her mind raced with thoughts on how she could avoid Selene and the physical contact. She was losing her mind. Run, she thought.

"Well, I hate to fuck and run, but thanks for another interesting evening. I think you're right, we wouldn't be good together. My apologies for bothering you, Selene." She stalked out, slamming the door behind her.

She practically ran down the hallway and out into the club. Her path clear, her mind starting to free itself from the shroud of strange fog. In her haste to leave, she bumped head first into a solid form.

"I'm sorry, I didn't see you," Francesca said, her head still swimming.

A strong hand grabbed her elbow before she fainted. "My fault completely, my dear. You look distressed, perhaps a glass of water?"

Looking up she faded into deep dark eyes.

"Oh not again." she said, recognizing the signs of what she suspected was a vampire.

Chapter Thirty-six

Selene felt like someone had kicked her in the stomach. Her feelings raced for Francesca. Grabbing her jacket, she ran after her. Knocking on the next door as she passed it, she yelled, "I'll be back. Keep an eye on Clarissa."

Clarissa opened the door. "Wait, Selene."

She didn't stop. She didn't look back. Instead she was focused on the man with his hand on Francesca, escorting her out the door of the club. Her senses spiked off the Richter scale. Whoever it was, he was a vampire and he had his hands on her girl. *Her girl? Oh great!* She didn't have time to flesh out her feelings right now. She needed to catch Francesca before something happened. In her condition, she was susceptible to a mere suggestion and that was Selene's fault.

"Francesca. Wait. Francesca!" Selene screamed at the pair walking toward the parking lot.

"Selene, wait. I don't think you should be out there alone," Clarissa yelled as she and Jax followed behind.

"Francesca, stop now," Selene commanded.

Selene could see Francesca trying to stop, yet the man kept pulling her along quickly behind him. Running, she yelled again at Francesca. She was gaining on the duo, reaching them just as the man dropped his grip on Francesca and bolted for the alley.

"Are you okay?"

"I think so. I don't know what happened. One minute I'm knocking into this guy and then next thing I'm being dragged behind him and unable to stop."

She wrapped Francesca in a quick hug she kissed her cheek. She let her go just as Jax and Clarissa reached them. "Jax, grab Francesca and get the ladies inside." She yelled and took off after the man.

"Wait, Selene…"

She heard Francesca yell after her. She wasn't about to let some low level bloodsucker get away with taking advantage of Francesca. She already felt awful, but she would have been devastated if something happened because of the way she treated Francesca. Clearly she was transferring her feelings onto this creep, but it would feel good to kick his ass for a reason and ease her own guilt. Maybe when she got back she and Francesca could talk. First things first, find the jerk and kick his ass. That would send a powerful message to anyone else who thought they could walk into her club and swoop in on unsuspecting women.

His scent was easy to follow. Down the alley, it dumped her into an open doorway. Without thought, she barreled ahead only to come face-to-face with the very man she was chasing.

De Marcus.

꧁ ꧂

"Ms. Lockwood." A whisper somewhere far off called to AJ "Ms. Lockwood."

There it was again. A soft voice, a nudge–someone calling her name, only it wasn't Clarissa.

"I don't think she's going to wake-up."

"I'll call her office and see if someone can meet us at the airport. Maybe I should call the police, she's beat-up pretty bad."

"I don't know but hand me those wipes, she smells awful."

AJ cracked her eyes barely enough to see the flight crew of her jet standing over her. Wetness wiped across her face and down her neck. Another swipe of wetness startled her.

"Stop, please," she barely eeked out.

"Oh, Ms. Lockwood, you're awake."

"Have we taken off yet?"

"Yes, just minutes ago."

She felt her world spin as she tried to sit-up. Her head throbbed with each beat of her heart. Touching her side she had some satisfaction that the wound had stopped bleeding and was slowly starting to heal.

"I need a phone."

"Of course." The attendant went to the front of the plane and came back with a cell phone. "Who would you like me to dial? Oh, wait…I'm sorry we don't have a signal."

"Why am I not surprised? Shit."

Closing her eyes, she leaned her head back and tried to swallow. "Water please."

"Oh, of course."

Her world just couldn't right itself could it? It would take at least an hour to get to the city, a half an hour to land and in the mean time she hoped she could get a signal so she might possibly be able to check on Clarissa. She examined her hands. The caked on dirt and blood needed to come off. Finishing the bottle of water, she tried to get up.

"Can you give me a hand, Tonya?" she requested.

"Are you sure you want to get up, Ms. Lockwood? I mean you look like you've been in a bad accident. Why don't we wait until we land? I'll call for an ambulance and we can get you checked out."

"I'm fine, really. I just need to wash this gunk off of me. I can't stand to smell myself for one more minute and I'm sure you're thinking the same thing."

"Oh no Ms.—"

AJ raised her hand, stopping Tonya. "I pay you well, but I don't pay you to lie, so if you'll just help stand. I want to wash-up."

"Yes, ma'am."

"There should be a few travel kits in the back. Can you see if you can scrounge me up something to change into?" AJ swayed a bit as she slowly made her way to the compact bathroom.

"All I could find were some sweats. Actually they're mine, but I'm happy to help out. I just don't think we wear the same size shoe." Tonya handed the clothing to AJ.

At least they weren't pink with sparkles. AJ shook her head.

"Thanks. I appreciate the clothes. Can you keep an eye on the phone and let me know when we have a signal. I need to make an important phone call."

"Of course. The pilot says we'll be landing in about twenty minutes. I'm sure we'll have a signal when we land."

"It might be too late by that time." AJ hated admitting it, but De Marcus had the jump on her. She would just have to hope that Selene was doing her part and keeping Clarissa safe. Looking down at the cell phone still nestled in her hand she noticed two small bars of availability.

Success!
She could finally call Clarissa.

Chapter Thirty-seven

Selene stopped just inside the door of the small room. It was empty except for De Marcus sitting in a chair staring at her and the man she was chasing standing next to him.

Fucking, De Marcus.

"Well, isn't this an interesting situation," he said, leering at her.

"A trap, how clever of you, De Marcus."

"Yes, well you fell for it didn't you?"

Selene could kick herself for being so possessive. The man she was after had put his hands on Francesca and all she could think was to kick his ass and save the girl. Oh, how chivalrous. Shit! Selene slipped her hands in her jacket trying to control her rage. She would kill De Marcus tonight, period. Evil like his deserved a brutal death and she was just the one to provide it.

"Now why would you want me?"

"Seriously? Selene, you're smarter than that, with you out of the way and AJ dead, I have Clarissa all to myself."

Selene gave De Marcus the best shocked expression she could muster. He had no clue AJ was still alive on her way to protect Clarissa. It wasn't her job to pop his little bubble, only to protect Clarissa. If she forfeited her life in that job, then so be it.

"Surprised? I thought you knew."

"How would I know?"

"Well, I thought Butch would call and gloat, but obviously I misjudged him. He has a modicum of class after all."

"So, where is Clarissa? Back at the club?"

"You don't think I'm going to let you near her, do you?"

"I don't think you're going to have a choice," he said. The door behind her closed and she heard the dead bolt slide. She was locked inside and the odds weren't in her favor at two against one.

Just as De Marcus pulled his hand from inside of his jacket, Selene pulled her stiletto from hers.

He gripped a grenade. That was original. If the grenade hit her, there was no way she could survive. It would blow her to pieces. Even a spoon wouldn't be able to scoop her up. He had thought of everything.

He nodded his head towards his company, who exited out of the only other door. Now this was interesting, he was going to do his own dirty work. Well, maybe she did have a chance. She looked around the room. Two windows, the back door and the front door, no furniture except the chair De Marcus sat on.

Selene flicked her stiletto open and smiled back at De Marcus. She wasn't going down without a fight and she hoped he knew that.

"You've got to be kidding me? You think you're going to kill me with that little pig sticker?"

"You think you're going to kill me with that?" Selene said, head nodding at the grenade.

The door behind De Marcus opened, causing Selene to shift her focus momentarily. In the next second, she heard the ping as the pin dropped to the floor and the click as the spoon of the grenade was released. De Marcus flung it towards Selene. She instinctively hurled herself at De Marcus. He flashed a wicked smile then launching himself across the room, his body aiming for the window. Selene grabbed De Marcus as he hit the pane and the grenade exploded behind them. A blast of splintering glass, broken wood and a flash propelled them across the lawn until they finally skidded to a stop. Selene straddled a cursing De Marcus, remembering a not too distant time when she was in this exact position.

An explosion of movement brought the two together. There was a swishing of the rapier as it cut the air, then flesh drifted through the breeze. A solid thud of a punch landing and an audible expulsion of breath echoed. Another thud, the blade cutting through cloth and the quick movements ended just as fast as they had begun. Selene found herself thrust upward at the end of De Marcus' arm. Her breathing was quickly being cut off, but her sword was buried to the hilt in De Marcus' chest. His grasp on Selene's neck gave way as he reached for her hand on the rapier.

Selene tumbled forward sending De Marcus onto his back, cushioning her fall. Landing on top of De Marcus, she felt a shooting pain in her arm. He had sunk his fangs into her forearm and held her against him.

"Release me, you son of a bitch," Selene shouted, pulling her arm from his clenched teeth.

Selene could see the blade of her rapier had bent and stuck out behind De Marcus's shoulder. Grabbing the handle she began to wiggle it back and forth opening the wound wider. While the blade was close to his heart, it wasn't a fatal wound. Nonetheless, it would keep him down for a few days. She continued to yank on the blade, blood soaking his white shirt. The action finally caused De Marcus to release his grip on her arm and he began to scream.

"I'll kill you, you bitch."

"Stop screaming or I'll continue to open you like a Christmas pig." Selene jerked the handle again to emphasize her point.

She felt De Marcus try to toss her off, so she reached down and pulled the dagger she had hidden in her boot and pushed it into his throat. The tip instantly drew blood and she licked his throat. A tingle rushed through her when his blood hit her system. She felt her body tighten and surge again. Setting her fangs to his jugular....

"Wow, I think we've been here before, De Marcus." Blood streamed down the side of her face, her words dripping with irony. Her head spun from the concussion of the blast. She was damn lucky to be alive and she would make him pay for trying to kill her. Her knuckles contacted with De Marcus' chin, forcing him sideways under her. He bucked, trying to dislodge her. Wrapping her legs around his hips she forced him down with her forearm pressing across his windpipe.

"Get the fuck off me, or you'll regret it." De Marcus spat out.

"Oh that's original. I think you said that, too." Selene choked on the smoke and dirt that filled the air, trying to take a deep breath. Her lungs hurt, her eyes burned, but she was alive.

"You're going to regret meeting up with me tonight, you bitch."

"Unless you've got a little friend in your pocket, I don't think I have anything to worry about." Selene wiped her face on the back of her sleeve, dangerously close to De Marcus' mouth. She needed to get the hell out of there, the blast would bring the police, and all the lookie-loo's.

"Never under estimate me you bitch." He practically choked on his words as Selene slid the stiletto across his face. Blood spurted from the wound, speckling her own face. She raised the tip aiming for his throat. As she thrust downward, he bucked his hips, sending the tip into his own eye. Selene jerked up, the tip dislodging his eyeball but not completely severing it from the orbital socket.

"My eye, you fucking bitch," he screamed.

Selene finished the procedure, flicking her wrist and tossing the eyeball on the other side of his head. His screams of pain pierced the cold air, echoing off the surrounding buildings. She would need to get the hell out of there before people came running to see the explosion. Sitting up on De Marcus's body, she drove the stiletto through his chest. She could felt his heart beating through the blade and into her palm. His energy pushed through her. She'd dreamed of this day for over a year and couldn't believe she was finally able to give Clarissa the peace that she needed. She would finally have her life start anew with AJ. Blood seeped up the hole in his chest and around her hand as she pushed the blade deeper.

He reached up grabbing a fist full of hair and tried to pull her off, but she didn't budge. He didn't have the strength to dislodge her and so she kept pushing all of her weight behind the thin slice of death.

"Die you bastard."

"Fuck you."

"Not today, De Marcus." Leaning on the knife

harder she said, "This is for all those women you destroyed, and all those innocent lives that you took. You're a sick bastard and now you get to meet the same fate they did, at the hands of another vampire."

"I won't die Selene. I'll be alive in all of those I turned. They'll hunt you down and kill you. They'll avenge my death."

"Don't romanticize your own death, De Marcus. Nobody gives a shit if you die. If they did they would be here to save you."

"You'll risk your ability to walk in the light just for revenge, Selene?" Blood spurted from his mouth as he tried to breath.

"Revenge is just like deceit, only it leaves a sweeter taste on your tongue. I'll let you know how it tastes when I see you in hell."

Without hesitating, she transformed and bit down on his neck, savoring the last of his life, draining it completely out of him. The smell of smoke, blood and something else, something dark filled her nostrils. His energy became hers and she shook, feeling his essence vibrate through her. No one was around to see him die, no one to see her rise victorious over his body. She stood alone in the darkness, blood dripping from her mouth. The sounds of sirens drawing closer reminded her that she didn't have much time. She slung him over her shoulder and carried his limp body further away from the chaotic scene unfolding behind her. Selene had waited so long for this day. She wasn't about to be denied the ability to make sure De Marcus was finally dead.

The sound of an explosion rocked the club, but no one dancing even paid attention. The bass of the music only added to heart rocking vibrations, but Clarissa and Jax stood looking at each other.

"What was that?" Clarissa grabbed Jax's arm and steadied herself.

"I've got a bad feeling."

"What's wrong?" Francesca asked.

"Nothing," they said in unison.

"Maybe I should go and see what happened?" Jax said tossing his head at the front door.

"We'll just wait here," Clarissa said, patting Francesca's hand trying to reassure the poor girl. She studied the woman, wondering what it was about her Selene found so intriguing. Clarissa hadn't met any of Selene's *friends*. That part of Selene's life was off-limits to everyone, including Clarissa and AJ. While she considered Selene a dear friend, she doubted Selene thought the same of her and AJ. They would always be just on the periphery of Selene's life, one foot in and one foot outside the boundaries that Selene set for herself.

"So how did you meet Selene?"

"Selene?"

"Yes, that dark and sexy woman I saw you intimately engaged with earlier."

The silence between the two women was voluminous considering they sat in a crowded nightclub. Clarissa waited as Francesca clearly seemed to measure each word before speaking. "Oh please, I've known Selene for a very, very long time. Probably longer than you've been alive—"

"Oh…you're…I mean, you and Selene are *old* friends?"

"Old?" Clarissa wasn't quite grasping the meaning of old, but the emphasis was there and she was sure that Francesca knew something she shouldn't.

"Well, I mean you look so young, you can't be that old, right?"

"Quite right, so back to the question, how did you two meet?"

Again, Francesca hesitated and Clarissa wanted to strangle the girl. It wasn't a trick question. Besides, why was she trying to make conversation with someone she was sure Selene was either going to eat or dump? Anyway, Francesca wasn't even Selene's type.

"Work."

"Work?"

"Hmm, work. I work for Lockwood Pharmaceuticals and she came into the office one day."

"Really?"

"Yep, she had business with the owner and we ran into each other at the office."

"I see," The world just became a little smaller imagining this slip of a girl working at Lockwood Pharmaceuticals, her Lockwood Pharmaceuticals. *Office staff. Really Selene, can't you do better than that?* She thought looking Francesca over.

"How do you know Selene?" Francesca threw the question right back at Clarissa.

"We meet years ago here in this very club," Clarissa answered. A wicked grin creased her face. She watched as Francesca put two and two together and seemed to fade at her response.

"Oh, I see."

"Don't worry dear, that was years ago, but we've stayed friends, sort of." Clarissa implied. She knew she was being evil, but for some reason she was jealous of having to share Selene with someone else. She had something Clarissa would never have, an innocence that made her appealing and she was sure that's what Selene found so attractive. She'd have no idea who Selene really was, what kind of danger she was in or that she could easily lose it all with just a bite.

A hush suddenly came over the club and then a murmur started. Clarissa and Francesca stood to see what was going on. The dance floor parted just as a woman weaved her way towards them.

"AJ," Clarissa said as she was swept off her feet.

Chapter Thirty-eight

Selene moved cautiously through the darkness. The back of her club was only a few hundred yards away. She felt different. Lighter. Scared. *Free.* She'd made a promise to herself only days earlier that if she killed De Marcus she'd stop working as an assassin and take her life back. Now, she had to fulfill that promise to herself and she wondered if she could. The strain of De Marcus both physically and emotionally weighed on her. Then there was Francesca. Walking away from this life would open up other possibilities for them. Was she ready for that?

Pulling keys from her ripped pants she unlocked the heavy door, swung it so hard that it slammed against the cement wall and bounced back hitting De Marcus's body as she peered into the dark storeroom. Flipping the light on with her elbow she balanced the body and reached for the cold storage door. She locked him inside for safe keeping while she got cleaned up and prepared to burn his body. It was the only way to make sure a vampire was dead never to return. She'd done it with others and now she would do it one last time, and this time it would mark the end of one life and the beginning of another. This time she would offer Clarissa the honor of torching the bastard who had made her life a living hell for so long. She deserved that much.

Slipping past the crowd in the club, she spotted

Clarissa, her arms wrapped tightly around AJ. Francesca sat at the bar, safe and enjoying a drink. She suddenly could only focus on Francesca. She could summon her, if she wanted. Bring her to her room and ply her with thoughts of rapturous love making, but she wanted Francesca to come willingly not through subversive thoughts or deception. Hanging her head she waited in the hall and watched Francesca interacting in the group. Was this what it was like to fall for someone? Did doubt always creep in and take over? Only moments ago she was self-assured, self-absorbed and arrogant. She could have any woman in the club tonight and yet the thought of Francesca rejecting her sat in the pit of her stomach.

Suddenly she needed to talk to Francesca, alone and now.

❧❧❧❧

AJ couldn't breathe. Clarissa held her tight and wouldn't let go.

"Sweetheart, please. You're hurting me."

"Oh my god. Look at your face. Are you all right?" Clarissa ran her hands over AJ's body. When she flinched at the touch on her side Clarissa pulled the sweatshirt up.

"Is that a bullet hole? Who shot you? When did you get shot? Where did you go?" Clarissa peppered her with questions.

"Slow down." AJ swayed a little and before she could move Clarissa pushed her onto a bar stool. "I'll be fine."

"Would you like me to look at that, Ms. Lockwood?" Francesca offered.

"Dr. Swartz, I didn't see you standing there. How are you? Better yet, what are you doing here?"

AJ felt Clarissa's gaze move from her to Francesca and back again. This time she was poking around in her thoughts.

"Don't do that," she said, looking at Clarissa. "She's an employee."

"I see."

"Do you my love? Jealousy isn't your color. Besides, you know I only have eyes for you." AJ moved closer to her lover and smiled.

"Well I feel stupid," Francesca whispered.

"Why's that?" AJ said wrapping an arm around Clarissa's middle pulling her closer.

Clarissa put her finger over AJ's lips. "Nothing, my love," Clarissa interjected. "We just found out that we have a few things in common."

Pulling Clarissa's finger off her lips she kissed the tip. "Do *we* now and what would that be?"

"Selene." Francesca and Clarissa said in unison.

"Where is Selene?" AJ cut Clarissa off.

Before they could say anything else, Selene walked from the back of the club. Blood matted her hair down against her face. She walked with a limp and she smelled of smoke and dirt. Francesca ran to her and grabbed her arm, helping her to a barstool.

"What happened?"

"I got into a fight with that guy who had his hands on you." Selene grabbed the bar to keep her from toppling over.

"Oh my god. Can I have a towel please?" Francesca ordered.

AJ stood, giving Selene her seat.

"AJ? When did you get here?"

"Just now. Hell, you look like I feel. I hope you got the better end of the deal?" Slapping Selene on the back, she smiled. Knowing Selene, the bastard was probably dead and deservedly so.

"Yeah, he's in the back storeroom."

"Who?" Everyone chimed in.

AJ waited while Selene ordered a drink, downed it, and then looked at Francesca and then answered. "AJ, can I see you in the back?"

The two walked away. Neither spoke a word until they were out of ear shot of the group.

"What happened?"

"De Marcus."

"What? Where?"

"He's dead." Selene tossed her head towards the storeroom. "He's in the back."

"No shit?"

"No shit."

AJ searched Selene's face and wondered what had changed. Usually she would have a swagger, a sign of a deed well done. Only this time she was reserved, quiet and solemn.

"You okay?" AJ grabbed her shoulder and started to knead the bunched muscle.

"Yeah." Selene looked over AJ's shoulder at Francesca.

"What happened at the coven?"

"Long story, I'll tell you later."

"We good?"

"Yeah." Selene kept her eyes on Francesca, never looking at AJ.

"Hmm, I see."

"You see what?" Selene questioned angrily.

"It's Francesca."

"It's nothing. I've done the job you hired me to do. We're even. I need a shower. I figured we'd take De Marcus out to the mine and burn him. I think we should let Clarissa have the honors since he was the bastard who took her innocence." Selene turned back towards the bar and then looked back at AJ. "You okay with that?"

"Yeah."

Chapter Thirty-nine

Francesca sat at the bar nursing a drink, watching AJ and Clarissa across the room catching up. She'd heard bits and pieces of their conversation. Enough to know that AJ was almost killed earlier, but survived because of her love for Clarissa. Why couldn't she find that kind of love? Would she be willing to give it all up for someone like Selene? Her life, would she trade it for an eternity of love? She wasn't sure she knew Selene well enough to give something so precious so quickly. Perhaps if they dated, got to know each other better. God, why did she always try to wrap everything in a nice little package and…. Her cell phone brought her back to reality.

"Hello?"

"Are you okay?"

She could hear the concern in Daphne's voice. Shit, she'd completely forgotten about her friend.

"I'm sorry, Daphne. I completely forgot to call you. Are you okay?"

"I'm good, I was just worried about you. A nice gentleman from the club brought me home. He made sure the apartment was fine and then left. I've been sitting here worried about you. When are you coming home?"

"I'm on my way now." Francesca conceded deep down inside that she wasn't going to be one of those women who threw themselves at someone who didn't want her.

"Good, I can't wait to hear how it went with tall, dark and sexy."

She heard Daphne giggling on the other side of the line. If she only knew, Francesca thought. "Well there isn't much to tell."

"Hmmhmmm."

"I'll catch a cab and see you in about fifteen minutes."

"Okay, see you them."

A soft touch on her arm turned her around. Selene stood close to her, smelling washed and a gentle smile reached her eyes.

"Can I take you home?"

Francesca panicked. "I don't think–"

"It's okay. I'll have Jax take you home."

She cursed herself. This was the opening she'd waited for, right?

"Wait, are you sure you have time? I mean AJ and Clarissa have been waiting for you, too."

"Do you mind if I take Francesca home? We can take care of that other business when I get back, if that's all right?"

"This is more important," AJ said, winking at Selene. "Go, take care of your business. That other stuff will wait till you get back."

"Thanks."

Francesca smiled at her boss. She wasn't sure what was going on between Selene and AJ but she was glad to have the opportunity to finally talk to Selene.

"Thank you." Francesca hugged AJ and Clarissa good-bye. "I'll see you at work."

AJ patted her side and said, "Thanks for stitching me up. I think I'll take a couple of days off. See you

Monday."

"Okay, see you Monday."

With that, she was out of the club and into the dark, cold damp night with Selene right behind her.

⁂

Selene opened the car door for Francesca, but stopped her before she got in.

"I'm not very good at this kind of thing…"

Before Selene could finish her sentence, Francesca melted against her. Her head buried against Selene's chest. Wrapping her in a tight embrace, Selene felt the world fall away, leaving them to each other. Tipping Francesca's chin up, she looked into soft, understanding eyes.

Light.

That's all she could think of when she looked into them.

"I can't promise you a lot, but how 'bout we take this one day at a time? I know we've sorta jumped the gun right into intimacy, but if you're willing to step back and start fresh, I'd like to do something I've never done before."

"What's that?"

"Fall in love."

"Never?"

"Nope, never."

Admitting that she'd never been in love made her feel vulnerable, weak and afraid she'd have her heart broken. Reaching into her pocket, she rubbed her thumb over her father's pocket watch. She could almost feel the engraving on the inside.

My love is like the air, always around you, embracing you. Love, M.

Epilogue

Selene dropped De Marcus's body on the gravel. Expecting him to come to life she poked him with the tip of her boot and then poked him again. Looking down at his face, she noticed his eye socket had sucked in where his eye used to be. Now she wished she'd picked that up, too.

"You ready, buddy?" AJ set the gas cans down next to his head.

"Yep." Selene stepped back and looked over at Clarissa, who hadn't said a word since finding out he was dead. "You okay, Clare?" Selene reached over and grabbed her hand, squeezing it reassuringly.

She just nodded and smiled weakly. They had all hoped they would find closure with De Marcus's death, but Clarissa deserved it most of all. Selene doubted she would find it anytime soon. Scars like these took years to fade and they would always lay just under the surface unable to be seen by anyone else, but you always knew they were there. She hoped her own scars would heal with time. Maybe they would with the love of a good woman like Francesca.

They had talked the whole way home and then stood at Francesca's front door for another two hours. The time had flown and suddenly it was daylight and Selene could still feel its warmth on her skin. She hadn't succumbed to the darkness, not yet at least. With a promise to take things slower, they'd made a lunch date. Agreeing that something more casual would be less stressful for both of them and less likely to find them rolling between the sheets. Was this how couples negotiated the dating landscape? She wasn't sure, but she'd talked to Clarissa while AJ made sure the quarry was closed and empty. Clarissa had been supportive and given her blessing. Not that Selene needed it, but Clarissa was the closest thing to a friend Selene had and they had history, an intimate history together. Selene respected that, plus it felt good to talk to her about Francesca.

AJ handed Clarissa the gas can, but she shook her head, so AJ doused his body. Each woman looked down at the man lying at her feet. Each wanted him dead for different reasons; one for taking her innocence, one for hurting her lover, and for Selene, well it was just a job. She knew the bastard deserved this and more, but this was the best he would get. AJ handed Clarissa a flare gun and they all stepped back. He lay at the edge of the quarry lip waiting for his final punishment. Whether he knew it or not, he would give Clarissa her life back tonight and for that Selene was grateful.

"Whenever you're ready baby," AJ said, lovingly stroking Clarissa's back. "I love you and he can never hurt you again. This is for your sister, your mother and your father."

Without another word, Clarissa raised the gun and shot at the body. Tears streamed down her face as she pulled the trigger. As soon as his body caught fire, she turned into AJ and buried her face into her chest. Selene and AJ stood watching his body burn. It flamed up and then burst into a bright fireball. De Marcus was finally dead.

"Let's go home, baby." AJ raised Clarissa's face up and kissed her.

Selene could only smile and pat AJ on the back as she watched her old life flame out and the promise of a new life burn bright.

"Let's go home ladies."

About the Author

Isabella, writing as Jett Abbott, lives in California with her wife and three sons. She teaches college, and speaks at high schools and universities on current issuses facing the LGBT community. She enjoys traveling with her wife, riding her motorcycle, and spending time with her family. She's also the owner of Sapphire Books Publishing.

She is a member of Gold Crown Literary Society, Romance Writers of America. She has written several short stories, and writing as Jett Abbott she is now working on the follow-up to *Executive Disclosure - Surviving Reagan*

You can follow her on Facebook at

www.facebook.com/isabella.author

or at the Sapphire Books website

www.sapphirebooks.com

Other **Isabella** titles available at Sapphire Books

Award winning novel - Always Faithful - By Isabella   ISBN - 978-0-9828608-0-9

Major Nichol "Nic" Caldwell is the only survivor of her helicopter crash in Iraq. She is left alone to wonder why she and she alone. Survivor's guilt has nothing on the young Major as she is forced to deal with the scars, both physical and mental, left from her ordeal overseas. Before the accident, she couldn't think of doing anything else in her life.

Claire Monroe is your average military wife, with a loving husband and a little girl. She is used to the time apart from her husband. In fact, it was one of the reasons she married him. Then, one day, her life is turned upside down when she gets a visit from the Marine Corps.

Can these two women come to terms with the past and finally find happiness, or will their shared sense of honor keep them apart?

Broken Shield - By Isabella - ISBN - 978-0-9828608-2-3

Tyler Jackson, former paramedic now firefighter, has seen her share of death up close. The death of her wife caused Tyler to rethink her career choices, but the death of her mother two weeks later cemented her return to the ranks of firefighter. Her path of self-destruction and womanizing is just a front to hide the heartbreak and devastation she lives with every day. Tyler's given up on finding love and having the family she's always wanted. When tragedy strikes her life for a second time she finds something she thought she lost.

Ashley Henderson loves her job. Ignoring her mother's advice, she opts for a career in law enforcement. But, Ashley hides a secret that soon turns her life upside down. Shame, guilt and fear keep Ashley from venturing forward and finding the love she so desperately craves. Her life comes crashing down around her in one swift moment forcing her to come clean about her secrets and her life.

Can two women thrust together by one traumatic event survive and find love together, or will their past force them apart?

American Yakuza - By Isabella - ISBN - 978-0-9828608-3-0

Luce Potter straddles three cultures as she strives to live with the ideals of family, honor, and duty. When her grandfather passes the family business to her, Luce finds out that power, responsibility and justice come with a price. Is it a price she's willing to die for?

Brooke Erickson lives the fast-paced life of an investigative journalist living on the edge until it all comes crashing down around her one night in Europe. Stateside, Brooke learns to deal with a new reality when she goes to work at a financial magazine and finds out things aren't always as they seem.

Can two women find enough common ground for love or will their two different worlds and cultures keep them apart?

Executive Disclosure - By Isabella - ISBN - 978-0-9828608-3-0

When a life is threatened, it takes a special breed of person to step in front of a bullet. Chad Morgan's job has put her life on the line more times that she can count. Getting close to the client is expected; getting too close could be deadly for Chad. Reagan Reynolds wants the top job at Reynolds Holdings and knows how to play the game like "the boys". She's not above using her beauty and body as currency to get what she wants. Shocked to find out someone wants her dead, Reagan isn't thrilled at the prospect of needing protection as she tries to convince the board she's the right woman for a man's job. How far will a killer go to get what they want? Secrets and deception twist the rules of the game as a killer closes in. How far will Chad go to protect her beautiful, but challenging client?

Titles writing as Jett Abbott

Scarlet Masquerade - By Jett Abbott
ISBN - 978-0-9828608-1-6

What do you say to the woman you thought died over a century ago? Will time heal all wounds or does it just allow them to fester and grow? AJ Locke has lived over two centuries and works like a demon, both figuratively and literally. As the owner of a successful pharmaceutical company that specializes in blood research, she has changed the way she can live her life. Wanting for nothing, she has smartly compartmentalized her life so that when she needs to, she can pick up and start all over again, which happens every twenty years or so. Love is not an emotion AJ spends much time on. Since losing the love of her life to the plague one hundred fifty years ago, she vowed to never travel down that road again. That isn't to say she doesn't have women when she wants them, she just wants them on her terms and that doesn't involve a long term commitment.

AJ's cool veneer is peeled back when she sees the love of her life in a lesbian bar, in the same town, in the same day and time in which she lives. Is her mind playing tricks on her? If not, how did Clarissa survive the plague when she had made AJ promise never to change her?

Clarissa Graham is a university professor who has lived an obscure life teaching English literature. She has made it a point to stay off the radar and never become involved with anything that resembles her past life. Every once in a while Clarissa has an itch that needs to be scratched, so she finds an out of the way location to scratch it. She keeps her personal life separate from her professional one, and in doing so she is able to keep her secrets to herself. Suddenly, her life is turned upside down when someone tries to kill her. She finds herself in the middle of an assassination plot with no idea who wants her dead

www.ingramcontent.com/pod-product-compliance
Lightning Source LLC
Chambersburg PA
CBHW051252210726
48287CB00002B/460